TO
ICEBERG

Also by W. J. Corbett

The Bear who Stood on his Head
Dear Grumble
Little Elephant
The Song of Pentecost
Winner of the Whitbread Award
Pentecost and the Chosen One
Pentecost of Lickey Top

W. J. Corbett
TOBY'S ICEBERG

Illustrated by Tony Ross

MAMMOTH

First published in Great Britain 1990
by Methuen Children's Books Ltd
Published 1992 by Mammoth
an imprint of Mandarin Paperbacks
Michelin House, 81 Fulham Road, London SW3 6RB
Reprinted 1992

Mandarin is an imprint of the Octopus Publishing Group,
a division of Reed International Books Ltd

ISBN 0 7497 0452 7

A CIP catalogue record for this title
is available from the British Library

Printed in Great Britain
by Cox & Wyman Ltd, Reading, Berkshire

CONTENTS

1
TOBY'S MISSION

Toby the young white whale lived in the cold sea just off the tip of Iceland. He loved his home very much. Every morning he shouted his happiness, sending the sea-birds shrieking and wheeling away in alarm. This special morning of his life was no different. The nervous birds poised themselves to flee as he opened his huge mouth.

'My name is Toby and I live in a lovely school of whales, and I'm the luckiest grandson living just off the tip of Iceland,' he cried at the surging sea and the sky. 'For I have the best grandad in all the ocean, who loves to join in my games and sing my song. I should be so lucky.'

After getting all the joy off his chest Toby paddled his plump body into position so that his blunt nose was lined up on the huge target of his grandad, who was basking peacefully a hundred metres away. Yelling 'charge' at the top of his loud voice Toby closed his wet brown eyes and set off through the water, his tail and flippers thrashing at full speed ahead.

'Great thundering icebergs. I've been scuttled,' roared Old Moby Dick as his grandson struck him square amidships in his barnacled belly. Rolling his eyes in anguish he caught sight of his gleeful grandson rocking in the waves nearby. The old whale's sigh was deep and long.

'Caught you napping again, Grandad,' grinned Toby. 'You didn't manage to get out of the way that time. Would you like to close your eyes and go back to sleep, and try again? Or would you rather sing my song with me instead?'

'I thought you were going to hunt down a whaling ship this morning,' said Old Moby, wearily. 'I thought you were going to float in wait for one to sail over the horizon, then charge and bash its sides in!'

'I only said that to catch you unawares, Grandad,' smirked Toby. 'And my plan worked, didn't it? You were all flummoxed when I charged and hit you in your midriff, weren't you?'

'I certainly was flummoxed, Grandson,' said his grandad, wincing in pain. 'But can we skip any more of your games for today, only I'm feeling a bit tender this morning, and I'm not so young as I was?'

'Okay, Grandad,' said Toby, brightly. 'We'll play tomorrow instead. In the meantime we'll sing the song I made up myself. Remember the rules now, you hum the tune in your deep voice while I sing the clever words. Are you ready... both together now...' and with much gusto Toby launched into his song, his fed-up grandad humming half-heartedly along:

'We all live in a lovely wavy sea,
A lovely wavy sea,
A lovely wavy sea,
We all live in a lovely wavy sea,
Wide enough for you and me...but not ships.'

'Did you enjoy humming my song, Grandad?' asked Toby, adding proudly, 'It took me ages to compose the words and the tune all on my own.'

'I've never enjoyed humming a song more,' said Old Moby, wheezing as he tried to catch his breath. 'There are a few snatches in it that are pure genius.'

'We'll sing it again then,' said Toby, pleased. 'But this time I'll let you hum "but not ships" all by yourself.'

'I think I've hummed enough for one day,' said the old whale, hastily. 'It's my humming pipes, you see. They're getting a bit rusty in my old age. How about enjoying a quiet snooze together?'

'Talking about "rusty", Grandad,' said Toby, ignoring him as his interest switched to something else. 'Will you tell me your life story again? About how you came to earn all those badges of courage all over your body? How you came by all those rotting ropes and rusty harpoons that festoon your scarred old belly and back. Tell me again about how you waged a solo war against the whaling ships in the adventurous olden days.'

'Not again, Grandson,' groaned Old Moby. 'If I've told you that story once, I've told it a thousand times.'

'No whaling ship would mess with you in your younger days, eh, Grandad?' boasted Toby, his wet brown eyes filled with hero-worship. 'Tell me again how you earned that special harpoon in your side, and how you went on to batter the evil ship that fired it. I'll start the story for you, if you like. "One day I was swimming along minding my own business when suddenly out of the mists came sailing..."'

'Another time, eh, Grandson?' pleaded the old whale. To get a bit of peace he resorted to trickery. 'Great thundering icebergs,' he gasped, peering over Toby's humpy back. 'Is that a ship I see sailing over the horizon? What's the betting it's a whaler disguised as a pleasure cruiser? Go get it, Grandson. Go bash its sides in before it sneaks round behind us and fires its harpoons.'

'No ships...no whalers in our sea,' yelled an angry Toby, swirling about in the water to scan the horizon through his wet brown eyes. Spying a suspicious-looking smudge that, in his opinion, had no right to be there he sped off like a torpedo to deal with the hated enemy, calling over his fat shoulder, 'Don't pine for my company while I'm away, Grandad. As soon as I've dealt with the whaler I'll be back to try to catch you napping again.'

'That's what I'm afraid of,' groaned Old Moby, gloomily watching Toby's bow-wave out of sight. 'Oh, for a moment's peace, that's all I crave. Nobody loves that lad more than I do, but oh, for a rest from his games and pranks, for frankly I'm too old and tired to cope with them any more. And if I have to hum that silly song once more...'

While Toby was searching the horizon for a whaler to bash, Old Moby was paddling his huge bulk through the icy sea to have a few words with Toby's mother. He found her scouring the calm waters in search of nourishment for her son's tea. Fresh squid and succulent seaweed and similar goodies. She was not pleased to be interrupted and scolded by her own father.

'Don't you think it's about time you found young Toby something useful to do with his nose?' he grumbled. 'You know I adore the lad, but I'm sick and tired of being rammed awake at all hours of the day. Then there's that awful song I'm forced to hum. What are you going to do about it, Daughter?'

'Nothing at all,' replied Toby's mother, annoyed. 'I've got quite enough to do feeding him four square meals a day. You're the one he loves the best and looks up to. You find his irritating nose something useful to do. Just tell him I love him and leave it at that.' And off she swam to attend to more urgent things.

Alone again the old whale pondered long and deep. Then suddenly the brainwave came to him. 'That's it, what young Toby needs is a goal in life,' he mused out loud. 'A goal in the form of a mission. Like I had when I was his age, when I made it my mission to send every whaling ship to the bottom of the ocean. And I have the perfect solution.'

Exactly one minute before tea-time Toby arrived back from the horizon. His blunt nose was creased with puzzle wrinkles.

'There was no sign of the whaler, Grandad,' he said, disappointed. 'The only thing on the horizon was a little black cloud. Perhaps you only imagined the whaler, eh? Anyway, on the way home I decided not to try to catch you napping, for it was getting on for tea-time. But I've got a good idea for some fun later on. After we've had our tea, you and me will set out to scour the whole of our Artic ocean for this evil whaler you might have imagined. And don't worry, Grandad, we'll track it down if it takes weeks. And if we get tired of searching in the midnight hours we can always sing my song to cheer ourselves up. Isn't that a good idea, Grandad? Right, I'll swim over to collect you when I've had my tea. I think it's fresh squid and luscious seaweed tonight...lovely grub.' And smacking his thick blubbery lips he made to swim off.

'Hang on one moment, young Toby,' said the old whale, sternly. 'Tea-time can wait for once. I want you to wallow quietly while I explain the mission in life I've planned for you. And don't grin and prepare to charge me, I'm not joking this time.'

'No jokes...just a mission?' said Toby, his wet brown eyes clouding over with boredom. But because he loved his grandad very much he obediently paddled alongside his hero to hear him out.

'Now, lad,' said Old Moby looking serious. 'At some stage we all need a mission in life. Playing games and singing songs is all very well, but there is also a serious side to life. My serious side was my war against the whalers.

We are now going to tackle your serious side. In short I am going to saddle you with a bit of responsibility. Now then, Grandson, I'm going to give you an order and you will obey it immediately, is that clear?'

'Yes, Grandad,' said Toby, lowering his huge head, his wet brown eyes no longer sparkling. 'You know I'll do anything you tell me.'

'There's a good lad,' said Old Moby, approvingly. 'Here is the order then. I want you to swim across to the Great Ice Pack and smash off the largest chip of ice you can. Do you think you're up to that task?'

'I'll smash off the largest chip ever,' boasted the young whale, his enthusiasm suddenly fired. 'What do I do then, Grandad?'

'You will float it back here where I'll explain the next step in your mission,' was the reply.

'More orders, eh,' whooped Toby, his chunky body churning around in the icy sea. 'I'm beginning to enjoy my mission already.' Seconds later his blunt nose was creating a huge bow-wave as he surged off in the direction of the Great Ice Pack a few miles to the north.

'It must be a large chip now,' warned Grandad. 'None of your sissy slivers. And if you see a whaling ship ignore it: you are now a whale on a mission.'

'Received and understood, Grandad,' shouted Toby over his lumpy shoulder. 'I won't

14

be two ticks. Hurrah for a mission in life,' he bellowed at the surging sea and the sky, scaring the sea-birds, who rose shrieking from Old Moby's back where they'd been enjoying a quiet roost.

'Moonlight already?' mumbled Old Moby, awakening with a start some time later. Then all at once the chilly night was shattered by a jubilant cry. Focusing his sleepy eyes the old whale was startled to find himself staring at a huge cliff of ice, its peaks and crags rearing ghostly white in the moonlight. It took him quite a while to collect his scattered senses.

'I've brought back the chip of ice, Grandad,' cried Toby, swimming from the back to the front of an enormous glittering prize.

'Great thundering icebergs,' gasped the old whale, trying to believe his eyes. 'I've seen some chips of ice in my time, but that must be half of the North Pole.'

'And it was smashed off completely by nose-power, Grandad,' said Toby, proudly. 'So what's your next order, Grandad? We can't wallow around admiring my iceberg all night. I've got my mission to get on with.'

'Indeed you have,' gulped Old Moby, pulling himself together. 'Now then, lad, your next order is to begin to push it south. Why south, you ask? Because many thousands of miles away, just over the hot equator, live our cousins. They are not lucky whales like us. For

15

water is scarce in those regions, and there are certainly no icebergs.'

'I've got your drift, Grandad,' butted in Toby, bursting with confidence and raring to go. 'My mission is to push my iceberg south to the equator for our parched cousins to lick at when they get very thirsty. So, have you some words of wisdom for me before I set off?'

'Of course I have,' stuttered Old Moby, still shocked by his grandson's get up and go, and fumbling for words. 'Grandads always have words of wisdom for grandsons who set out on missions. I will give you the same advice my grandad gave me when I swam away to make a name for myself. So here it is: always keep your head up high and keep your nose clean. And beware of hangers-on, they'll try to take you for a ride. But being such a little know-all I bet you'll recognise a hanger-on from thirty nautical miles away.'

'Of course I will, Grandad,' fretted Toby, champing at the bond of love that still bound them close together. 'Don't worry, Grandad, I'm taking all your wise advice on board. So give me your blessing and I'll be off.'

'God bless you, Toby, my grandson,' sighed the old whale, suddenly realising how much he would miss him. A tear crept from the eye of a sad old whale.

'Don't weep, Grandad,' soothed Toby. 'I know you want to hum my song before I go. So,

for the last time before I return home famous…'
The shivery Arctic air shook to the sound of
Toby's 'wavy sea' song, the last notes and
words shouted and hummed defiantly as a
warning to all whaling ships to steer clear of
Toby's sea while he was away on his mission.

'When you miss me very much you can
always hum my song to yourself,' said Toby,
much moved. 'Would you like to sing it again
before I go?'

'Shouldn't you be on your way, Grandson?'
replied Old Moby, hastily. 'We wouldn't want
you to miss the southward flowing tide. After
all, a young whale on a mission scoffs at
lingering.'

Toby eagerly agreed. But there was still one
more matter that needed to be dealt with before
he set sail for the south. 'Grandad, don't you
think I should apologise to Mother for
skipping tea tonight? She'll also want to bless
me before I go. I do hope she doesn't weep and
wail all over the place when she hears about
my mission.'

'You're right, Grandson.' So, leaving the
mountain of ice rocking in the silver seas the
pair swam over to the blowing school to
confront her.

'Of course Toby has my blessing,' she
snapped. 'I just hope that when he returns
home famous from this mission he'll be
considerate enough to be on the dot for tea. I

will bless him, but if he's one second late from the equator his meal will go to the sea-birds like today's tea just did.' So saying, amid the shrieks and the flapping of scoffing sea-birds she plunged into the depths to organize supper for other young whales in the school...the kind who would have the good manners to turn up for it on time.

'I wonder what my friends will be having for supper?' said Toby, wistfully. 'I know Mother's a bit sharp-tongued, but she's marvellous at providing good, filling, blow-out grub.'

Alone again he and his grandad wallowed together in the frosty waters just off the tip of Iceland, the iceberg looming high above them.

'Not blowing cold on the mission, are we?' enquired the old whale. 'I remember times when I went without a square meal for weeks. My mission was what counted. If you want to cry off...'

'Not on your life, Grandad,' cried Toby, full of vim again. 'If the great Moby Dick could go without tea for a few weeks, so can his lucky grandson.'

Wishing the old one a loving farewell Toby swam to the north-side of his glittering prize and began to nudge it south with the end of his blunt nose. Soon he and the wall of ice were creating a bow-wave of speed in the tradition of all worthy missions. In no time at all the young white whale and his iceberg had vanished beyond the curve of the southern horizon.

'Great thundering icebergs,' breathed Old Moby softly, alone with the roosting sea-birds again. 'I thought I was a bit of a Jack-the-lad in my younger days, but that lad puts me in the shade when it comes to true grit. But then it's in his blood, of course. Now for a good night's sleep with no worries about being shocked awake in the morning by a thump in the belly. And no more having to hum that silly song, thank heaven. So come on, old Moby Dick, let's dream about our swashbuckling yesterdays, and never regret that the perils of the wide ocean will be tackled by young Toby and his like. Here's strength to his nose, and also a prayer for his safe return home in time for tea one day.'

2
A SEA SERPENT SINGING

A week later found Toby still swimming strongly, his iceberg firmly under control. It was as if the sparkling gift for his cousins in the south was glued to the tip of his nose as he battled the waves that tried to break his spirit. But Toby had spirit in plenty, even though he hadn't tucked into a tasty tea for days. Meanwhile the sun was getting warmer and higher with each passing hour. The iceberg was beginning to sweat just a mite.

Suddenly, just as Toby was breasting yet another cresting wave, he was surprised to hear someone singing in the surf nearby. The singer

21

sounded very sorry for itself as it sang a very sad song:

'Why am I always shouting goodbye
And never shouting hello,
Where is the joy in my tears when I cry,
Please tell me for I don't know?

Why am I always saying, "So long,"
And never, "Oh, do stay to tea,"
Where are the friends who belong in this song,
Won't somebody please tell me?'

'I'll tell you this, whoever you are,' said Toby, swimming around to the south-side of his iceberg and easing it to a stop. 'If you'd cease moaning and give me a chance to say hello then I wouldn't need to say goodbye so soon. So where is this tea that you are inviting me to? I've missed mine for the last seven days.'

'What would you say to squid for starters, and sea-urchins for afters?' replied a delighted voice.

'I would say, "Lovely grub",' answered Toby, his fat belly rumbling hungrily. 'But if we're going to enjoy a meal together, don't you think we should introduce ourselves? I'm Toby, grandson of the famous Moby Dick, so who are you? At the moment you're just a swirly patch of foam with a sad voice in the middle.'

'If I surface will you promise not to shout

goodbye and flee in horror?' said the owner of the miserable song. 'Only it's happened so many times before. My looks tend to frighten folk away. It's not fair, I've got such a lovely kind personality when you get to know me.'

'Nothing frightens me, not even whaling ships with harpoons at the front,' boasted Toby. 'So hurry up and show yourself, my precious. I'll tell you just how precious after the scrumptious breakfast-tea you've promised me.'

Instantly the patch of foam began to boil. Suddenly from the centre emerged a knobbly head topped with two sets of horns. A long forked tongue flicked between dagger-sharp teeth. This very ugly head was perched on top of a scrawny neck festooned with seaweed. Also rising from the sea, Toby could see the humps of a snake-like tail equipped with saw-blade spines, the sting at its tip wagging a warm welcome at the young whale. All these horrifying parts belonged to a rainbow-coloured sea serpent with yellow eyes that gazed pleadingly at Toby for friendship and understanding. The lonely creature was revealed. Because of his ugliness he was forced to enjoy tea-time all alone. But Toby was made of stern stuff. He formed his own opinions about folk, no matter what they looked like. And Toby liked what he saw.

'Well, Serpent,' he said, admiring his

brilliant colours. 'Have I shouted goodbye yet? So hello and when do we get stuck into our lovely grub? I'm absolutely famished.'

With a cry of delight and tears of joy streaming down his ugly cheeks, the serpent dived down to his deep-sea pantry. He soon returned with enough squid and sea-urchins to feed two kings. And the young whale and his new friend dined on their breakfast-tea-time till they were near fit to bursting. When there was nothing left to scoff the serpent became weepy again.

'Why does tea-time always have to end?' he sobbed. 'If only we could start tucking in all over again. Now we've polished everything off you'll soon be burping goodbye, and I'll be alone again.'

'What an unhappy serpent you are,' burped Toby, pityingly. 'Are you worried that I might think you're one of those hangers-on my grandad warned me about? Well, never fear, I like your lovely kind personality. But as your first best friend I must point out your glaring fault. It has nothing to do with your looks. It's your song, I'm afraid. It's much too sad to attract folk to swim in to tea. What you need is a happy song with a cheerful hello in the melody.'

'How can I sing about hello when the whole of my life has been one long goodbye?' the serpent wept, his yellow eyes streaming tears again. 'Since my parents waved me goodbye many centuries ago, the only thing that never shuns me is the end of my tail. That's why I've been swimming round and round in this patch of foam all my life.'

'Shouting hello at the tip of it,' finished Toby, understanding. 'Because your tail is the only person who doesn't think you too ugly to take tea with.'

'That's it...exactly it,' cried the serpent, deeply moved that such a young white whale could care the least jot about him. 'Oh, if only you would stay and share tea with me for ever and ever.'

'I've a much better idea,' said Toby. 'Because I've enjoyed our magnificent meal, and because I've enjoyed your magnificent company, and because I think you are magnificently shaped and coloured, I'm going to shake you out of your magnificent rut with the offer of a magnificent job. How would you like to share my mission in life with prospects in the south?'

'Me...share your mission in life?' shouted the serpent, writhing with happiness in his broth of froth, his yellow eyes alight with hope. 'And will my new job entail inviting lots of folk to stay for tea?'

'Your tea-parties will be packed out, I promise,' said Toby, grandly. 'Throw in your lot with me and my mission, and the rest of your life will be one long hello.'

At this point the serpent went quite haywire with excitement. 'Please describe my job to me,' he begged, lashing the sea with his stinged tail.

'There will be hard work ahead,' warned Toby, indicating his parked iceberg with a wave of his large flipper. 'You must have noticed that I didn't drop in for tea quite by myself?'

'I have been wondering about that,' admitted the serpent, eyeing the gigantic wall of ice parked nearby. Then his ugly face dropped as he voiced his sad thoughts, his yellow eyes dripping tears again. 'I knew it was all too good to be true. You are going to tell me that the iceberg has been following you since you first set out for tea at your grandma's. And you want to be rid of it. And my new job is to shout hello at it, so it will scoot back north where it belongs…?'

'Certainly not, Serpent,' interrupted Toby, indignantly. 'I am pushing my iceberg south to the equator where my cousins are lying parched and belly-up through lack of water. My mission is to give them the lick of life before they die of parchness. Your job is to help me push it there. So how strong is that knobbly nose of yours? Can it push day and night through fair weather or foul? Do you think you are up to the job, Serpent?'

'My nose was born to push,' cried the serpent, his yellow eyes dancing with happiness again. 'Just tell me where to place it and I'll have our iceberg moving at the speed of light in seconds flat...'

'Steady,' urged Toby, calming him down. 'Iceberg-pushing is very hard work, as you'll soon learn. A gruelling journey like ours must be full of hope and cheer, which means your sad song is out for a start. So, Serpent, are you prepared to learn and sing my song every push of the way? If so, the job is yours.'

'All right, give me some singing lessons,' pleaded the desperate serpent.

'You also have to mind my iceberg if I'm called away on urgent business,' cautioned Toby. 'For instance, if a whaling ship appears on the horizon and I need to dash off and batter its sides in, would my iceberg be in the same spot when I returned?'

'To the very centimetre,' promised the serpent, stoutly. 'Our iceberg would remain as steady as the Rock of Gibraltar in the stormiest of seas.'

'In that case the job is yours,' said Toby, happy to have made such a wise choice of pushing partners. 'We will now tackle the singing lessons. Listen closely as I sing my song on my own. Then we'll sing it together.' And the young white whale opened up his huge mouth to belt out his favourite song, his tubby body twisting in the water to the beat of:

'We all live in a lovely wavy sea,
A lovely wavy sea,
A lovely wavy sea,
We all live in a lovely wavy sea,
Wide enough for you and me...but not ships.'

'What a beautiful song,' lied the serpent as Toby looked proudly at him. 'I'll bet you made it up yourself.'

'Only every word and every note,' said Toby, puffing out his fat chest. 'My famous grandad, Old Moby Dick, especially loves it. In fact he hates to sing anything else. So, Serpent, are you ready to sing it with me?'

The serpent, desperate for a job, winced only a little bit as he joined in.

The serpent knew just where to place his nose on the iceberg to achieve full pushing-power without catching frostbite. In no time at all the mission was ready to continue the long journey southwards. To the happy strains of, 'Wide enough for you and me...but not ships,' the enormous lump of weeping ice moved majestically from its berth, firmly pushed and guided by the noses of two extremely close friends.

Completely content in each other's company the days passed serenely for the pushing pair.

As often as possible they paused to take tea together, always singing Toby's song afterwards. The only blight was the appearance of a whaling ship on the horizon. Toby would leave the iceberg in the serpent's charge and set off in a blur of tail and flippers to bash its sides in. When he returned he sheepishly had to admit that all he had tackled was another little black cloud. So on they travelled with scarcely a ripple disturbing the indigo waters that smoothed their passage south.

But still the iceberg wept. As the sun and the sea became warmer and warmer, so disturbing things continued to happen to Toby's glittering gift for his cousins in the south. Its gentle perspiring was now a lathered sweat as rivulets of water began to stream down its sides. The serpent was afraid to draw Toby's attention to it in case he was sacked from his first job for insolence. As for Toby, he blissfully refused to see any problem. In his wet brown eyes the iceberg was still as pristine and sparkling as the day he'd set out. It would take fresh eyes and a more brave and critical soul to point out the obvious problem. But in the meantime the two friends continued on their way, one clinging to the only companion he'd ever known, the other clinging to an image of the perfect iceberg, smashed sweet as a nut from the Great Ice Pack two thousand miles of time and sea ago.

3
THE STORMY STOWAWAY

High in the sky the stormy petrel circled the iceberg and its pushers again, his beady black eyes weighing up the situation. For days now the bird had been flying out of sight of land, nursing a severely sprained wing. He desperately needed somewhere to rest until it healed. Unable to bear the pain any longer he threw caution to the wind and soared downwards.

'Permission to come aboard, Captain,' he croaked, skidding in to land on Toby's blunt nose. He sighed. 'Ah, the bliss to take the weight off the old wings. Thank the Lord for the kindly captain you surely are.'

'Permission to come aboard denied,' shouted Toby, his wet brown eyes crossing as they tried to focus on the cheeky bird. He didn't notice the stowaway's drooping wing, or he would have spoken more kindly. And the bird was too proud and cocky to moan about his ailments.

'So, shall I throw myself overboard?' the grinning bird suggested. 'What happened to the Code of the Sea? What happened to good old hospitality?'

'What happened to politeness?' Toby shot back. 'It's hardly good manners to request permission to come aboard when you already have. And on the end of my nose, too. The nose of the grandson of the famous Moby Dick is hardly a landing and launching pad for birds without manners.'

'So why don't you shout goodbye and fly away,' said the angry serpent. 'Because you'll get no hello's from me and my friend.'

'If that's your attitude I'm staying tight,' replied the bird, digging his sharp claws more firmly into Toby's blubbery nose. He cocked his head to one side, his black eyes mischievous. 'By the way, who's the composer of that rubbishy song you keep singing? Don't tell me, I can guess.'

'I am, if it's any of your business,' flared Toby. He rolled over in the water to dislodge the stowaway, but the bird was used to duckings and wasn't thrown in the least.

'Anyway,' said Toby, growing angrier and angrier. 'What would a common duck know about music? My grandad Old Moby Dick thinks I am a musical genius, and he should know. He knows everything.'

'Steady on the "duck",' protested the stormy petrel. 'I've never waddled anywhere in my life.'

'Except off the end of my nose,' Toby shouted. 'So be off with you, and don't try to talk about music. There are folk in this ocean who would be glad to share tea with a musical genius such as me.'

'Like me, for instance,' said the loyal serpent. 'Toby's song is a perfect song to sing after a heavy tea-time.'

'Well, I say your song is rubbish, and in my opinion, you two are disturbing the peace of the sea,' replied the stormy petrel, spiritedly. 'Now, if you want to hear some real singing, just listen to my song,' and opening his sharp beak the lame bird began to trill.

'North, south, east and west,
That's the place I love the best,
Homeward bound on the nose of a whale,
That's the way I love to sail,
Stowed away, the right tide caught,
Heave to starboard,
Pull for port. . .but not ships.'

'How's that for a number one hit song?'said the bird, all preening and breathless. 'I made it up on the spur of the moment while perched here on the end of your nose.'

'And you had the nerve to call my song rubbish,' scoffed Toby. 'As music, yours is pure gibberish. How can you love north, south, east and west all at the same time? Your emotions would be torn to tatters if you tried. And how could you heave to starboard and also pull for port without going in zig-zags completely off your course? As a hit song, yours doesn't make sense, Stormy Petrel.'

'It doesn't even rhyme at the end,' cried the angry serpent. 'Probably because the cheeky stowaway pinched "but not ships" from the end of our much better song.'

'Ouch, there's a sharp rap on the beak,' mocked the bird. 'I get the feeling I'm not welcome aboard this vessel.'

'No you're not, so less of the back-chat,' snapped the serpent. 'Just remove your claws from my friend's nose and hop it. And don't hover about in the hope of being invited to stay for tea. This mission likes to take its meals in private.'

'Very well, you leave me no choice,' announced the stormy petrel. 'I suppose I must swallow my pride and throw myself on your mercy. Did you notice how I was trailing a wing when I came in to land?'

'Are you saying that you're injured, and that we are being unkind?' said Toby, shocked. 'But why didn't you say so at once?'

The bird shrugged. 'I thought everyone was familiar with the Code of the Sea which plainly states that all seafaring folk must help another in distress.'

'And a very good code it sounds,' replied Toby with feeling. 'Please accept my humble apologies. You see I've lived a very sheltered life just off the tip of Iceland and am quite unworldly about such a beautiful code. It's strange my grandad Old Moby Dick never told me about it. . .but then he was always too busy enjoying my games and singing my song. Though he did say, during our long talks, how he longed to get a serious word in edgeways. So, of course you can heal and gather strength on the end of my nose, poor little bird.'

'And you can stay for tea,' said the serpent, looking ashamed of himself. 'For I've quite fallen in love with the code myself. And don't try to protest about sharing our meal, my friend and I won't take goodbye for an answer.'

'Changed your tune, eh? Hello's all round, eh?' grinned the bird. He smacked his beak. 'So tickle my taste-buds with something tempting.'

'How do you fancy squid and fresh green kelp for afters?' said the serpent, drooling at the thought.

'Throw in a herring or a mackerel and I'm yours for life,' replied the eager bird, his beady black eyes sparkling.

'Done,' shouted the serpent. He immediately sank beneath the waves to raid the ocean's plentiful larder.

The three were soon enjoying a scrumptious tea in the shadow of the iceberg, the waves of the dreamy green sea lapping around them.

'So, where are you pushing this fast-melting iceberg to?' asked the bird, wiping his beak on Toby's nose to get rid of the herring scales. 'Not too far, I trust? I suppose you know that icebergs don't travel well when the weather starts warming up. To be honest, I was surprised to see one this far south.'

'What do you mean "fast melting"?' said Toby, indignantly. 'My iceberg will easily make the journey to the equator intact. So long as we keep up our fast pace my cousins in the south will have plenty to lick at when we arrive.'

'Not if you keep stopping for tea all hours of the day,' warned the petrel. Then he had an idea. 'What this mission needs is a pilot. If you are dead set on reaching the equator before the iceberg melts then I must tell you that your steering is way out. If you keep to your present course you'll end up in China. So let's make a deal. You provide me with a free passage home and lots of nourishing teas, and I'll make sure we arrive at the equator in the shortest time possible. What do you say?'

'I say it's a bargain,' said Toby, quickly. 'China is quite out. My grandad said nothing about ending up in China.'

'In that case we'll start the little bird's singing lessons,' said the serpent, happily. 'Listen closely, Stormy Petrel, we'll sing it the first time and you can join in the second time.'

'Join in the second time what?' said the puzzled bird.

'My song, of course,' answered Toby, impatiently. 'You must forget the song you made up on the spur of the moment on my nose and learn my proper one. My song is happy and harmonious, and ideal for a long journey. That's the condition you must accept if you wish to join my mission. Take it or leave it, Stormy Petrel.'

'I knew there'd be a catch,' said the bird, good-naturedly. 'So, okay, warble away.'

Needing no further prompting, Toby and the serpent threw back their heads and sang their 'wavy sea' song with all the stops pulled out, and a few tears as well. Only a wandering albatross passing overhead complained about the terrible din. But burdened with the bearing home of a lost soul, that sad bird had little time for music. The lame stormy petrel, however, had. In no time at all he was cheerfully trilling Toby's song, word and note perfect. A short time after that he was flapping lopsidedly upwards to perch on the topmost tip of the iceberg. Tucking his sprained wing beneath his downy belly, he swivelled his sharp beak like a compass-needle until it pointed south – with just a teeny bit of north and east and west thrown in, for he loved all four points equally.

'There's a fair backing wind springing up, Captain,' he cried down to Toby. 'And the tide is running like silk. Cast off, let's make some fast knots south.'

'Aye, aye, Mr Pilot,' called Toby, excitedly.

After much heaving and grunting he and the serpent got the iceberg on the move again. The mission had barely travelled ten nautical miles before it ran slap-bang into a terrible storm. The three were dashed against the sharp edges of the iceberg by roller-coaster waves. Fierce bolts of lightning and rumbles of thunder flashed and clapped around them as they fought the raging elements, all sense of direction gone.

'Serpent, pray to God this isn't the end of our mission,' cried Toby above the uproar of dashing waves and surf. 'But if we are parted by the fury of the storm, goodbye my faithful friend, at least we tried to reach our goal.'

'I will never say goodbye,' yelled the serpent, clinging desperately to the wallowing iceberg. 'Just hang on, we'll see this through some-how. The storm must pass, and I'm sure we'll be laughing hello again in calmer seas.'

Just when it seemed that Toby and the serpent and the iceberg looked set to be ship-wrecked on different shores, the sound of a song came trilling through the racket of the storm. Or rather bits of two songs cobbled together, for the singer liked to be contrary:

'North, south, east and west,
We all live in a lovely wavy sea,
Homeward bound on the nose of a whale,
Room enough for you and me. . .but not ships.

It was the stormy petrel revelling in his favourite kind of weather. He began to shrill down instructions to his friends as they tried to control the rearing and plunging of the precious chunk of ice.

'All hands to starboard, Captain,' he yelled. 'Bring her around and trim your barnacles, Mr Mate.'

'Aye, aye, Mr Pilot,' chorused Toby and the serpent, glad to obey an expert on storms. Swimming swiftly to the starboard side of the iceberg they heaved with every ounce of strength they had left in their bruised noses. Then they trimmed their barnacles as best as they could. Slowly the enormous bulk began to swing round on a safer course.

'Belay there. The east wind is veering around to the west and blowing north,' shrieked the

bird, enjoying himself as never before. 'Bring her round so that her port-side faces her starboard-side. Look lively now, and don't forget to shiver your timbers.'

'Aye, aye, Mr Pilot,' cried the straining crew as they battled down below.

'Okay, steady as she goes,' ordered the pilot bird. 'How are those binnacles and barnacles?'

'Binnacles stowed and barnacles trimmed, Mr Pilot,' cried Toby and the serpent, anxiously poised to streak to a new trouble spot. But just as quickly as it had arisen, the storm subsided. Suddenly the ocean resembled a sheet of green glass again, broken only by the odd, playful whitecap breaking over the noses of Toby and the serpent as they wallowed gasping in the brilliant sunshine. Soon the beating of their hearts returned to normal.

'Break out the herrings, Mr Mate,' rapped the bird, his eyes twinkling as he returned to perch on Toby's nose. 'I think I've earned a good tea, don't you?'

'You certainly won't get a herring out of me,' bristled the serpent. 'What you will have is two herrings and one mackerel. As the hero who saved this mission it's all you deserve. Take it or leave it.'

'I'll take it,' the hero-bird grinned, smacking his beak in his usual, hungry way.

'And mind you shout hello when I return,' warned the serpent, warmly. So saying he

41

turned turtle and dived beneath the sea, to rustle up a rewarding tea for three very close friends.

While they were waiting for their meal, Toby and the bird had a little talk. The bird noticed that the young white whale looked agitated. Waddling up Toby's nose, the petrel thrust his cocked head close until his beady black eyes were centimetres away from Toby's wet brown ones. For a cheeky stormy petrel he was suddenly extremely sincere – his grin was only half its normal size.

'Get it all off your chest, young Captain,' he urged. 'What troubles you? Tell your old Uncle Pilot all about it.'

'It's all these teas,' said Toby, trying to hold back his tears. 'I love the serpent very much, but he keeps persuading me to stop for tea any time of the day or night. He doesn't seem to realise that I must deliver my iceberg to my cousins in the south in the shortest time possible.'

'Because of its melting state,' nodded the sympathetic bird. 'Well, that's icebergs for you. One day they're there, the next day they're not. I'm afraid only a sharp frost will save your iceberg from dieting away to nothing, and sharp frosts in these warm seas are rare as . . .'

'I don't mean that at all,' interrupted Toby, indignantly. 'My iceberg will easily make the journey to the south intact. But I want to complete my mission and rush home to Grandad who must be pining away for me. How would you like to be an old grandad pining away because he hasn't got a grandson to play games and sing songs with?'

'How would I like to be an old whale with lots of peace and quiet. . .hmm. . .that's a hard one,' said the bird, his grin at full stretch again. Then he was serious again. 'So what can I do to help?'

'If you and me bolt down our tea as quick as we can, then rush back to our sailing positions, the serpent will have to follow suit,' said Toby, pleadingly. 'And then when he suggests we stop for tea the next time, we can say we're not hungry. We'd gain a lot of sailing time. Will you help, Stormy Petrel?'

'Of course I will,' comforted the bird, deeply moved. 'Why, I think I'd rather starve myself to death than keep you and your beloved grandad apart one second too long. My, but you are an oddity in this cynical world, young whale. Youngsters who care so deeply for the old are as refreshing as. . .'

'As refreshing as the delicious tea we are about to enjoy,' cried the serpent, emerging from the depths in a broth of froth. 'Hello. . .hello. . .so what have you two been talking about? But never mind, what do you think of this feast. . .?'

It was a feast indeed, but over much too quickly for the disappointed serpent. After a good tea he liked to linger and lick, and chat and the like. In astonished bewilderment he watched the petrel gulp down his herrings and mackerel, wipe his messy beak on Toby's nose, then flutter lamely upwards to his look-out point. In shocked dismay he watched Toby cram his whole portion of squid and sea-urchin into his mouth, burp loudly, then swim rapidly to his pushing position on the iceberg. It happened without a word being spoken. Were his friends trying to tell him something, thought the crestfallen serpent? But he didn't have time to ask because the bird was already trilling down sailing orders, and Toby was pushing with all of his might. Mystified, and feeling a bit hurt, the serpent considered going on strike. But he'd promised Toby he never would. So he went back to work.

Guided by the enthusiastic pilot the iceberg wended its wobbly way towards the distant equator. Soon the mission was dipping below another horizon, an orange sun setting on a purple sea casting romantic plays of light upon the cliffs and crags of the lumbering block of ice. But the gathering darkness hid from view the rush of water and slush that flowed faster and faster down the iceberg's crumbling sides. But for Toby there was no problem. All he wanted was to carry out the orders of his beloved grandad and hurry back for their happy reunion in that faraway home just off the tip of Iceland.

4
SALMON
SCALES

'Reduce speed, reverse engines, obstacle ahead,' yelled the stormy petrel from his slushy perch. 'I'm afraid there's big trouble up ahead, Captain.'

Alarmed, Toby and the serpent plunged around to the front of the iceberg. Jamming their noses against it they strained every sinew to bring it to a ponderous halt.

'What obstacle? What big trouble, Stormy Petrel?' cried Toby, anxiously. 'I thought you were an expert pilot? What have you steered us into?'

'Perhaps it's the kind of obstacle that likes to drop in for tea,' suggested the hopeful serpent.

'Unless it's the kind of barrier that likes to shout goodbye, and pass us with its nose in the air.'

'It's the "passing" I'm worried about,' shouted back the bird. 'For I regret to inform you that this mission has just run into the Silver Streak. Which means that we'll be marooned in the doldrums for ages, forced to listen to an even sillier song than our own.'

'What sillier song?' said Toby, taking offence at the slur on his own. He craned his ears. 'I can't hear a sillier song. All I can hear is the babbling of the sea that seems to be getting louder and louder.'

'And even louder,' grimaced the serpent, his polka-dotted ears twitching sensitively. 'I hope it doesn't get too loud to bear. Unless the Silver Streak is babbling hello, of course.'

'Get ready to have your ears split,' yelled the stormy petrel. 'Oh, I could snap my beak in frustration. If only we'd arrived here a few hours sooner we'd have beat the Silver Streak to the crossing. But now it's too late, they're already swimming across our course. It's that serpent's fault. He delayed our progress one tea-time too many. Now what do we do?'

'My fault?' said the serpent, looking astonished and bewildered and hurt again. 'Doesn't everything stop for tea?'

'Never mind your hang-ups,' the bird snapped down. 'The fact is we have blundered into the Silver Streak, and I advise our captain to look ahead, and view the situation for himself.'

Mystified, Toby stood on his tail as Grandad had taught him. To his mortification he saw in the sea ahead a streak of silver advancing from the western horizon to the east. And it wasn't babbling, but singing. . .singing as only ten million voices can when raised together in determination and hope. For Toby could now hear the song. It was no babble. It was tuneful and filled with meaning. . .warning too:

'Don't hurry us we're salmon crossing,
Don't flurry us we're salmon crossing,
Don't worry us we're salmon crossing,
Crossing for the spawning grounds.'

'We demand our right of way as spelled out in the Code of the Sea,' bellowed a pompous fat salmon, also standing on his tail as he glared at Toby. 'Try to barge through my orderly ranks and I'll tell your grandad. I know who you are. And I also know that Old Moby Dick is the kindliest whale who ever swam in an ocean. So, be warned, young white whale, advance not one wave closer.'

'Excuse me, Sir Salmon,' replied Toby, indignantly. 'As the grandson of Moby Dick I absolutely respect the Code of the Sea. All my mission requests is that your Silver Streak

crosses to the spawning grounds as quickly as possible. Only my friends and I are bound on an urgent dash to the south. So can I politely enquire how long it will take your tidy columns to cross over?'

'Three days, give or take,' shrugged the traffic-control salmon. Then he bristled. 'But it will take much longer if a bunch of hoodlums from the north try to crash that crumbling lump of ice through our ranks. For then we'd have to re-form all over again, and that would cost the said hoodlums an extra three days of bored waiting about, at least.'

'Excuse me, sir, but we are not hoodlums, and nor is my iceberg crumbling,' flared Toby. 'We are earnest travellers concerned with delivering this mint-condition gift to my parched cousins to the south. All we are asking is that you speed up your crossing over, that's all.'

'Hoodlums indeed,' snorted the serpent, angrily. 'That is one salmon I will never invite to tea.'

'And I'll also remind you, Salmon, sir,' snapped Toby. 'My grandad might be the kindliest whale in the ocean, but he's also very quick to anger if he scents unfairness. If he knew how you were treating me and my mission he'd come crashing down here very fast to sort you out.'

'Steady, Captain,' soothed the stormy petrel,

alighting on the young whale's angrily wrinkled nose. 'Self-important salmon always get stroppy about missions bigger than their own. They hate being small fish in big ponds, you see. That's why they chase jobs in traffic control. Big-headed salmon love lording it over others.'

'Very well,' shouted Toby at the glaring, puffed-up salmon. 'Because you suffer from big-headedness I forgive you. But remember, Old Moby Dick is my grandad not yours, so he'll always take my side. And now, Sir Salmon, I would like to point out that this mission is not in the business of making waves. Because we respect the Code of the Sea we agree to heave-to for three days. Though I can't understand why you won't give-and-take, and pass across our course in two days and a half.'

'If I say three days, I mean three days,' bellowed the fat salmon, as stroppy as ever. 'So be warned, dicker half a day with me and I'll order my charges to take a fortnight to pass over to our holy rivers.' So saying he spun on his battered tail and addressed his millions of brothers and sisters in a rousing voice. 'Attention, Silver Streak, let's tell this bunch of hoodlums where we're at. What are we, and where are we going. . . ?'

His answer came swiftly and full-throatedly back:

'Don't dally us we're salmon crossing,
Don't tarry us we're salmon crossing,
Don't harry us we're salmon crossing,
Crossing for the spawning grounds.'

Chanting their song over and over the vast stream of silver fish continued to pass before the gloomy mission members, sparing them not one sympathetic glance. For as every salmon knew, their 'mission' was a question of life or death as their song plainly explained.

'That's it then,' groaned the stormy petrel. 'Now we have to endure three days in the doldrums having to listen to that racket. I say we should batter our iceberg through their ranks, and hang the Code of the Sea. May I be blunt, young Captain?'

'Of course you can be blunt,' said Toby. But his wet brown eyes looked very worried indeed.

'But not too blunt,' said the serpent, sharply. 'Otherwise someone will be going without tea, and others will be shouting goodbye to that someone.'

'Nevertheless, bluntness is called for here,' said the defiant bird, bluntly. 'At the risk of being pushed overboard I say we can't afford a delay. We have all noticed the rivers of meltwater streaming down the sides of the iceberg. And my look-out point is awash. I'm up to my shanks in slush up there. Let's face it, the gift for the whales in the south is melting at an alarming rate. And meanwhile the sun is getting hotter and hotter. So, young Captain, I say we must smash through the salmon ranks to save this mission from complete disaster.'

'I know you are right, and yet you are wrong,' despaired Toby. 'If only I knew what my grandad would do in this situation.'

'Kindness would come first with your grandad,' said the serpent, firmly. 'Though he would make short work of a whaling ship, he'd never crash through a tide of peacefully crossing salmon. Especially so near to tea-time.'

'You are right, Serpent,' said Toby. He addressed the frowning bird. 'I know you mean well, Stormy Petrel, but I'm determined to respect the Code of the Sea. I know my iceberg is perspiring a little. But aren't we all feeling hot and bothered after all the pushing and piloting? I think we should all cool down and rest up until the salmon have passed over. Is that clear, Mr Pilot?'

'As clear as crystal,' said the petrel, humbly. 'It's the pain from my sprained wing and waterlogged feet, you see. The discomfort is making me say cruel things I don't really mean.'

'Well, that's settled then,' said the serpent, his yellow eyes sparkling. 'So, as we are marooned here for three days I suggest we enjoy a three-day tea-time. Shall I dive down and rustle up something tasty? And will you shout "come back soon" if I do? And will you both weep "where could our friend have got to" if I'm a few seconds late surfacing?'

'You know we'd shout both those things, Serpent,' said Toby, kindly. 'But your idea raises a problem. If we tuck into tea for three solid days, won't we feel too over-full and under-fit when we continue our journey..?'

But the happy serpent had already vanished to dredge the deep for delightful things to eat. And this time he was confident that the meal wouldn't be bolted down, and there would be lots of time to talk afterwards.

Rocking gently in the soft waves, the mission members began to tuck into their huge, three-day meal. Meanwhile, another problem was raising its handsome head.

5
A SHARK'S LAMENT

'That's funny,' said the bird, cocking his head to one side. 'The Silver Streak has suddenly started singing out of tune. To my knowledge salmon never sing out of tune. And what is that big-headed, fat fish yelling about?'

'Murder, cold-blooded murder,' the plump salmon was crying, standing high on his tail again, his eyes wide in horror. 'Please help us. . .there's a killer on the loose tearing holes in my tidy ranks. Someone is mocking the Code of the Sea and scattering us far and wide.'

'Someone scattering the Silver Streak?' gasped Toby, choking on a mouthful of squid.

'What cold-blooded killer would do such a thing?'

'Only an utter rotter,' interrupted a silky voice with a built-in smirk. 'I just hope the bounder is caught. I'll certainly keep my eyes peeled for him. By the way, does my fin look straight to you? Only I think I've developed an ugly kink in it, and I worry a lot about my looks. Vanity, of course, but that's the price one pays for being a much admired megastar.'

Suddenly, something black and sharp and sinister zipped across Toby's line of sight. The young white whale felt all at once very frightened.

'Who is that speaking to us?' he cried, his wet brown eyes hypnotised by the cut and dash of the triangular tail.

It was the multi-coloured serpent who nervously suggested what the intruder might be. And he was right, for suddenly the black fin stopped dead in the water a nautical wave away from Toby's puzzled nose. All at once the owner broke surface wearing on his triangular face the widest and sickliest smile the young whale had ever shuddered at.

'Shark, shark,' yelled Toby, drawing his tender flippers close to his tubby body out of harm's way. 'And he's smiling directly at me. I'm only a young white whale in charge of a peaceful mission, so why is he smiling straight at me? Now he's winking. Why is he winking at me, and at nobody else?'

'Because he knows his smarm won't work on me,' said the serpent, sourly. His stinged tail was poised to strike as his yellow eyes stared jealously at the shark's handsome face. Pettily he added, 'Just look at all those rows of gleaming white teeth. Why are sharks so flashy? Good looks aren't everything.'

'Too true,' agreed the petrel, waddling up Toby's creased brow out of reach of the shark's gleaming white teeth. 'Show me a pretty face and I'll show you a treacherous mask. In my experience the wider the smile, the colder the heart. And if that shark who is smiling at our captain isn't the salmon-killer in question, then how come he's got a salmon stuck between his front teeth? And what's the betting his answer is a lie? Hello, he's stopped smiling. Get ready for the excuses and the blarney.'

'It was all a tragic accident,' butted in the shark, dissolving in tears. 'It was all because of my obsession for cold figures. I just happened to be counting the crossing salmon when one got stuck on my smile. Then, all of a sudden, the big fat one started shouting "murderer" and glaring at me.'

'Which was bound to interrupt your arithmetic studies,' said Toby to the groans of the serpent and the bird. 'Well, that sounds innocent enough. And I suppose you swam across to my mission to escape the false charges hurled at you? And you want us to give you the benefit of the doubt? No wonder you're upset, Shark. And by the way, your handsome fin hasn't got an ugly kink in it. It cuts through the water as pretty as a picture.'

'Thank you so much,' said the shark through his tears, his smile dazzling bright again. 'I knew the grandson of the famous Moby Dick would grant me a fair hearing.'

'Did you now?' answered Toby, pleased. 'So tell us more about your unfair life.'

'Well,' blubbed the shark. 'It all started when I discovered I had a talent for maths. I loved watching and counting things. But when I tried to make friends with nice warm fishes, they swam away and said they hated my cold hobby. Then a few days ago I began to shadow your warm mission. And how I longed to pluck up the courage to ask if I might become a member. . .to be part of something noble and good. But my shyness prevented me. And I was afraid that you would hold my passion for arithmetic against me. But, oh, how I longed to press my nose against your iceberg as mission member number four. How I wished that I could help you push it the remaining one thousand and seven hundred miles, seventy metres, and twenty-three centimetres to the equator.'

'My, you are good at sums,' remarked Toby, admiringly. 'Are we really so close to our goal?'

'Did you say "our" goal?' cried the shark, delightedly. 'Does that mean you are offering me membership in the mission? I will sing for joy if you are.'

'Oh, you sing as well, then?' said Toby, his interest broadening. 'What in particular — ballads, folk-songs, hard-hitting protest tunes. . .what. . . ?'

'Just the odd, sad lament,' admitted the shark, biting his lip with impossibly perfect white teeth. 'You'd hate my songs. You'd say, "Where is the joy in them?" Don't ask me to sing, for it will only make me cry.'

'It makes me cry to listen to our captain being bamboozled,' shouted the angry stormy petrel. 'But it makes me weep even more to watch him nodding sympathetically at that smoothie.'

'Too right,' cried the serpent, equally furious. 'How could anyone believe a word of that shark's sob-story? Handsome he might be, but what kind of vicious creature can sing sad laments while gorging on innocent salmon?'

'My grandad once told me, "Always give everyone a fair hearing,' said Toby, firmly. 'And that's what I'm going to do in the case of this shark. We'll soon know whether he's genuine or not after he's sung us a sad ballad. So, sing us a snatch of one, Shark.'

Shushing his irate friends Toby wallowed

comfortably in the glassy green water and waited for the newcomer to do his stuff. And the shark, his film-star face screwed up in pain and anguish, did just that. It was a self-pitying song. A song perfectly composed to melt the heart of a young white whale who tried to see good in everyone, in spite of their reputation:

'Why am I always a shark on trial
Because I have a charming smile?
Dismissed as vile
And full of guile,
Because I have a certain style?
Why am I always a shark on trial
Each time I flash my charming smile?'

'What a sad lament,' breathed Toby as the last, sour notes died away. 'I'm beginning to think you've been misunderstood all your life, poor shark. Yet you smile so beautifully when you really should be frowning. I can't imagine how you manage to be a wizard at arithmetic while also counting the blows life has dealt you. I think you should be welcomed amongst numbers less cold than your own. In other words, welcome aboard my mission as its newest member.'

'I protest,' shouted the frightened and jealous serpent. 'I won't have a shark smiling at me in the dead of night while I'm trying to sleep. I warn you, I won't prepare tea for him if he joins our mission.'

'That would be bad manners, Serpent,' said Toby, gently reproving.

'Then call me bad-mannered too,' cried the stormy petrel. 'I'd sooner walk the plank off the end of your nose, young Captain, than travel south in the company of a probable killer.'

'That would be mutiny, Mr Pilot,' said Toby, sternly. 'And you said yourself "probable killer". Well, the shark hotly denies the charge. Which means that we must give him the benefit of the doubt. So, no more griping, for our new companion must be eager to have his first singing lesson. You do realise that only my song goes, Shark? Are you ready to forget your own sad ballads and sing only my song for the rest of the journey south?'

'Who needs to learn it?' replied the delighted shark. 'After shadowing your mission for so long, your lovely music is engraved on my heart. I hope you'll forgive me for learning it without permission?'

'Your keenness does you credit, Shark,' said Toby, flattered. 'And I'm sure skill with arithmetic will make the beat of my song sound even better. And so, all that remains is for us to wait out the three days of salmon crossing before we head south once more.'

'Again, there's no need,' grinned the shark, his smart fin cutting rings in the green sea as he dashed around in excitement. 'As an arithmetic expert, I reckon that by juggling a few figures I can get this mission moving again in six minutes and thirty-five seconds flat.'

'Could you really?' gasped Toby, astonished. 'You can do that with a bit of complicated adding, multiplying, and taking away?'

'Certainly,' said the eager shark. 'And no one will ever know where the missing numbers went. It's merely a question of arranging the ranks of the salmon to create a blank column. Then all our mission has to do is simply slip through the numberless gap.'

'I'm protesting again,' warned the serpent. 'The sums of that shark send a chill through my bones. I'm convinced he's only offering to work out our problem in order to enjoy a good tea of his own.'

'What's the use of our protesting?' sighed the petrel. 'Our innocent young captain is determined to see good in the wicked. It's a pity his grandad didn't stuff some common sense into his head instead of playing rough games and singing silly songs.'

'My grandad loved my games and songs,' snapped Toby. 'Anyway, I'm only "hoping" to find good in our shark. When he swims over to the Silver Streak to perform his arithmetic magic, I'll be swimming alongside him in case he's tempted to fiddle the figures. Now are you both satisfied?'

'No,' answered the serpent, pettishly. 'I still think you are being dazzled by a beautiful smile.'

'Nor am I satisfied,' joined in the bird, rattling his beak in temper. 'The three of us were doing very nicely until old smarmy chops came gliding along.'

'Well, I'm sorry but my mind is made up,' replied Toby, stubbornly. 'I'm going with our new mission member to help him tussle with his tables, if he needs me. You don't mind if I come along, Shark?'

'Why, I wouldn't go without you,' said the shark, smiling sweetly. But suddenly he had stopped circling, his film-star face gazing at the horizon. 'But, oh, what a pity you'll be busy elsewhere.'

'Busy elsewhere, where?' said a suspicious Toby.

'Busy chasing down that whaling ship with the harpoon at the front,' cried the shark. 'Can't you see the smudge of smoke on the skyline? Now look directly beneath it. Can't you see the ugly shape of a whaling ship?'

'The smudge of smoke looks like a little black cloud to me,' argued the serpent. His yellow eyes flashed angrily. 'What ship? I see no ships.'

'It is a little black cloud,' agreed the bird, confidently. 'Our captain surely won't be taken in by the shark's obvious lie.'

But Toby was in no mood to listen to his friends. The word 'whaling ship' had brought about an astonishing change in him. All at once his tubby body took on the sleek lines of a killer torpedo as he revved up his tail and flippers. 'No ships. . .no whaling ships in our oceans,' he cried. Closing his wet brown eyes he charged full pelt towards the distant horizon.

'Which reminds me of my own urgent business,' grinned the shark. He slipped away towards the salmon lines murmuring, 'Problems, problems, always problems. . .'

'Well, we know what's going to happen now,' said the serpent, bitterly. 'Murder is about to be committed while we do nothing.'

'So do something,' said the bird, his webbed feet slipping and sliding on the rapidly shrinking iceberg. 'Or are you going to stay a tea-taking ninny all your life. . .?'

'Murder and mayhem. . .mayhem and murder. . .' floated the voice of the broken-hearted, fat salmon across the water. His distress was echoed by millions of terrified, babbling voices.

'I'll show you what kind of ninny I am,' cried the serpent. 'Do you think I'd lounge around thinking up menus while over there the Code of the Sea is being mocked? Tighten your belt, Petrel, for tea will be late today. . .' So saying he whipped around in the water and set off in pursuit of his handsome enemy, his sting-tipped tail poised to strike.

He arrived to view a scene of terrible carnage.

'Heaven help us,' moaned the despairing salmon, looking the serpent up and down. 'We appeal for a champion and they send a ninny. Oh, what's to become of my poor, suffering charges. . . ?'

'I'll show you all what kind of ninny I am,' roared the infuriated serpent. His yellow eyes flashed fire as he spied what he sought. With a cry he lunged at the surprised, happily munching shark, knocking out the killer's front teeth with one mighty blow from his spiny tail. Such was the serpent's fury, he continued to rain blows on his cringing enemy, the next tea-time being the last thing on his mind as all his frustrations burst forth.

Meanwhile, far away from the ding-dong of battle, Toby was angrily searching the sea for the hated whaling ship. But apart from a little black cloud drifting dreamily by in the sky, the only movement he saw was the gentle rocking of waves. Disappointed, he turned and swam back to his marooned mission. As he approached he was dealt the greatest shock of his young life. For Toby it was time to face the truth.

A blood-red sun was setting over the ocean as he swam slowly round and round his once tall and mountainous iceberg. Once so pristine

and proud, it now resembled a rather sad pancake as it continued to weep into the sea. Watched by the bird and the serpent, plus the shark, all looking uneasy for different reasons, Toby, the grandson of the famous Moby Dick lowered his blunt head and also wept. For the first time in his happy life he was experiencing unhappiness. He was no longer the confident youngster who had breezed from his home in the far north, convinced that his mission would be a doddle. He felt very alone and desperate indeed. For now he had no comforting grandad to swim to for advice as his hopes and dreams dripped sadly into the sea.

'Don't give your neck, down-hearted Captain,' called the bird, wading through slush as he leaned to peer kindly down at Toby's dispirited bulk. 'We can't give up now. Not having come so far. And there is one small ray of hope. Thanks to the shark who got his sums right, there is now a gap in the salmon lines just wide enough for what's left of our iceberg to pass through. We still have time to salvage something from our noble mission.'

'You've solved our problem, Shark?' cried Toby, brightening a little. 'Have you really gained us precious time to deliver even a much smaller iceberg to my cousins in the south?'

The shark was no longer wearing his charming smile as he muttered something inaudible. This was because the serpent had ruined his film-star face by knocking his front teeth out. Also his once jaunty fin drooped lop-sidedly in the water, looking very swollen and bruised. Wobbling unsteadily in the water he cast nervous glances at the glaring serpent.

'Oh, he solved the problem all right,' snapped the serpent, angrily. 'But at what cost? Look towards the salmon ranks and judge for yourself.'

Puzzled, Toby stood on his tail and peered. By the light of the moon he could just make out a multitude of salmon thrashing in silvery tumult as they frantically tried to re-form, to repair the gap torn in their once-orderly ranks. Yet still they sang their song of hope. Gazing at that pathetic scene, Toby sadly came to realise that his trust in the shark had been misplaced. Averting his eyes, he sank back into the sea, his plump body cradled by its gentleness. This latest shock had finally broken his already low spirits. But the spirit of the stormy petrel was as blithe as ever.

'Captain,' he cried, tapping urgently on Toby's closed eyelids with his beak. 'What's done is done. We can't bring back the poor figures that went missing from the salmon columns. And the serpent has punished the shark for his dastardly crime. So let's finish what we've started, even though our iceberg is a shadow of its former glory. Don't give up, young Captain. I'm sure your old grandad would wish you to press on, even if we arrive at the equator with nothing left to push. But you'd better make up your mind quickly, for the gap in the Silver Streak is closing fast.'

'The bird is right,' shouted the serpent. 'I say we skip tea tonight and steer for the south at full-speed ahead.'

'And what do you think, Shark?' asked Toby, shaking his sad head at the one who had let him down so badly. 'You begged and lied to be part of our mission. Do you still wish to see it through? And will you dedicate your efforts to the memory of your poor victims? And will you promise never to violate the Code of the Sea again?'

The shark managed a gap-toothed, weak smile. 'Okay, I'll turn over a new leaf. Arithmetic was beginning to bore me anyway. I've a mind to become a sporting shark and play teasing games of tag with little fishes instead of counting them. So let's forgive and forget and forge ahead, eh?'

'If I may protest yet again,' flared the serpent. 'We all know what he means by playing tag with little fishes. Any more of his lies and I'll "tag" him in the teeth again. I still say we should banish him from this mission.'

'I forbid any more falling out, Serpent,' interrupted Toby, sharply. He addressed the bird who was poised expectantly on the end of his nose, and ordered, 'Hop back aboard the remains of my iceberg, Mr Pilot. Give us a fix on the brightest star in the southern sky and guide us through that gap. And as we sail through I want every member of my mission to dip his nose in silent respect and grief for the suffering the salmon have gone through.'

'Did we deserve what we received. . .all the murder and mayhem. . . ?' sobbed the hollow-eyed traffic-warden as the shamed and bowed mission sailed through his tattered gap. 'Our mission was just as important as yours. From the bottom of my broken heart I curse that figure-fiddling shark. May all your tails droop to the side and propel you back where you started.'

His accusations and curses could still be heard as the mission sank below another horizon on the last lap of its journey to the equator.

'We all live in a lovely wavy sea,' hummed the shark through the gap in his front teeth. He got no further.

'Sing one more note of our lovely song and I'll loosen the rest of your smile,' warned the irate serpent. 'Don't you feel any remorse for the chaos you've left behind?'

'The song grates on my nerves too,' objected Toby. 'I don't think I'll ever feel like singing it again. For I'm dreading the sneers of my cousins in the south when they see the state of the iceberg that was meant to quench their thirst. Yet I must complete my mission. As the bird said, my beloved grandad would expect it of me.'

'Whoops. . .that's the spirit. . .whoops. . .' cried the bird. He kept shouting 'whoops' because he was having trouble keeping his balance on the dwindling lump of ice. It now resembled a large snowball, and like all things round in shape kept rolling over and over in the sea. Having to nurse a sprained wing was bad enough, but now the petrel was forced to become a circus acrobat as he rapidly adjusted his feet to avoid being spun off into the water.

But in the meantime the mission ploughed steadily on through the calm green seas. But the pushing was pretend now. To keep each other's spirits up, Toby was pretending to puff and blow, the serpent pretended to pant, while the shark, entering into the game, pretended to strain and wheeze. His wheezing emerging as a high-pitched whistle through the space in his once-perfect front teeth. On and on they swam in harmony, the seas they had left so far behind cleansing and washing all sins away.

6
THE MIRTH TWINS
AND SADDER NOTES

The tropical sun was searingly hot on the back of a young whale used to chilly, northern climes. The sea that lapped his belly was scarcely more cooling. No clouds marred the bright blue sky to threaten rain. Remorselessly the heat beat down on the mission toiling south through the blue-green ocean. And how longingly Toby yearned for the snapping frost and the warm company of his grandad far to the north. But he bravely shrugged off his homesickness and paddled on.

'There it is. . .straight ahead. . .the equator,' yelled the stormy petrel, skidding excitedly along Toby's nose. He had abandoned the 'iceberg', it being no bigger than a large hailstone by now. To keep the party cheered up he threw in a joke. 'Those of you who've never crossed the equator before might feel a downward, bumping sensation. Don't be alarmed, it's simply because the southern sea is lower than the northern one. So, prepare to be shook up, for you've been warned.'

Toby nervously steeled his plump body. So did the excited serpent. The tea-loving soul had never been so happy since leaving his swirly patch of foam, and was looking forward to being shook up in the southern ocean. The shark just giggled. He wasn't so easily taken in by corny jokes, he being wise to most of them himself. To Toby's disappointment the crossing of the equator was as smooth as could be. Nor was the serpent much impressed.

'Never mind,' he said to his young friend, his yellow eyes sparkling. 'We've crossed over, that's the main thing. Which I think calls for a celebration tea. So what would tickle your taste-buds?' He was just about to dive down and raid the foreign sea for exotic grub when Toby gave a loud yell of shock and surprise. The young white whale had suddenly felt a rising sensation in his midriff. It felt as if someone was trying to lift him out of the water and juggle with him.

'Put me down, whoever you are,' he cried, his heart in his mouth. Plunging his head under the water he tried to spot the culprit. But his vision was clouded by a curtain of waving green weed. Then, just as quickly as it had started, the pressure on his belly ceased. It was as if the 'someone' had given him up as being too heavy to lift.

'Now someone is trying to juggle me in the air,' yelled the serpent, his coils in a tangle, his yellow eyes flashing with fear. To his relief he too was rejected as being too ungainly to cope with. Though feeling all shook up from his experience, suddenly a smile spread over the serpent's beautiful-ugly face. He had a notion that his enemy the shark was next for the high jump. And his notion was right.

'I know who you are,' roared the enraged shark as he was lifted bodily from the sea and spun round and round like a top. 'And I warn you, put me down at once, otherwise I'll re-arrange you by putting your nose where your tail is.' His threat was heeded. He was instantly released to fall back with a crash into the water, his head spinning dizzily, his dignity in tatters.

'I told you these visitors from the north wouldn't appreciate a juggling act,' sighed a sad, piping voice from somewhere or other. 'Everyone knows that folk from the north like jokes and riddles best.'

'Nonsense,' boomed another voice, its tone full of bubbly fun. 'Folk from the north aren't at all intellectual. What they like is lots of knockabout stuff. Just listen to 'em applaud when I perform my death-defying, over-my-shoulder leap routine. Here we go, and notice, folks, I use no nets.'

Suddenly from the ocean burst a sleek, silver dolphin with a comically bulbous nose. As he soared upwards the dolphin winked a blue eye at the astonished Toby before performing a perfect, over-the-shoulder backwards somersault, nimbly knifing, nose first, back into the sea again.

For a long moment a stunned Toby and a shocked serpent gazed at the water as it calmed once more to its former, glassy stillness. They didn't have to wait long for what they were waiting for. Just long enough for the dolphin to believe that he had them clamouring for more. All at once his large head appeared with a silky 'glug', his blue eyes peering cheerfully at them. Two seconds later there sounded another silky 'glug' as a tiny sardine surfaced beside the dolphin's clown-like nose.

'I thought it was you two up to your tricks,' scowled the shark. 'I thought we'd bump into your nuisance sooner or later.'

'So who are these nuisances?' asked Toby, intrigued. 'And why all the juggling and leaping and winking?'

It was the sardine who replied. Grandly waving a tiny fin he introduced himself and his companion. 'May I present — appearing by popular demand for a seventh Farewell Comeback Performance – your very own. . .the much-loved Mirth Twins.'

'Hurrah, hurrah, encore, encore,' cried the delighted dolphin, applauding himself. 'We have come out of retirement to make you forget your troubles. So let us, the famous Mirth Twins, astound you with our brand-new comedy act that will make your sides split with laughter. In our time we've giggled our way round the seven seas, isn't that right, twin?'

'You betcha,' enthused the titchy sardine. 'Japes and jokes and juggling, that's us. You ain't seen nothing yet.'

'But let my twin demonstrate his own juggling skills,' boomed the dolphin, flashing another blue-eyed wink at the astounded Toby. He glanced around. 'Ah, yes, that will do. Go for it, partner. . .slay 'em. . .who says we're too old and past it. . . ?'

Before a horrified Toby and an appalled serpent could stop him the short sardine had darted through the water and had hoisted the pitiful scrap of ice that had once been a proud iceberg, on to the end of his nose. Proudly the small fish began to spin it round and round, faster and faster, the strong southern sun flashing rainbow colours from its pitted surface. And Toby, deeply hurt, broke down and wept at the sight.

'What kind of funny comedians are you?'

stormed the serpent. 'How dare you mock all that my young friend has striven for. Do you realise how long he's laboured and struggled to sail that iceberg into these southern seas so that his thirsty cousins could have something cool to lick on? Admittedly there is little of the iceberg left. But there's no call for you to rub it in. If your idea of comedy is to twirl someone's dream on the end of your nose, then I hate all comedians.'

'Those two. . .comedians?' scoffed the petrel. 'Like the shark I also know them well. They are the pests of the southern seas with their lust for fame. And they aren't even twins. They're just a couple of sea-roving failures with a strong sense of very bad taste in jokes.'

'And I intend to challenge that taste,' said the shark, gliding grimly forward. 'Unless they can save their miserable lives by really making us laugh?'

'Please,' pleaded the dolphin, hurriedly. 'My twin and I didn't mean to be cruel. We didn't know that the kind young whale was on a mission. We are sorry for twirling the remains of his iceberg, truly we are. So, to make amends, we would like to tell you a rib-tickling riddle. A good riddle always puts our audiences in a happy mood, doesn't it, twin?'

'You betcha,' agreed the sardine, his red-rimmed eyes blinking nervously. 'So kick off with it while we've still got 'em quietened and not throwing things.'

Needing no prompting the frightened dolphin launched into the riddle. 'Tell me, small partner, what do you call a pair of twins born to different parents, who look nothing like each other, who argue and fight all the time, and who shout, "Be quiet," when the other twin says something stupid?'

'I don't know,' piped the sardine, trying to look puzzled. 'So what do you call such twins?'

There was a long and awkward pause. 'I've forgotten my next line,' the dolphin hissed. 'It's that shark. . .he keeps glaring at me.'

'Why did I ever team up with you?' cried the angry sardine. 'Every time we face a hostile audience you dry up. I think we should break up this act and go solo on our own. For if you don't want fame, I do.'

'Oh, be quiet, junior twin,' said the dolphin, crossly. 'You know you are much too little to make it as a star on your own. Anyway, I've remembered my line now. I just hope that when it comes to your next line you don't forget it.'

'Oh, be quiet,' snapped the sardine. 'You worry about your lines, I'll worry about mine. So snap yours out so that I can deliver the punchline.'

'I won't,' replied the dolphin, peevishly.

'And why won't you?' cried the sardine, exasperated.

'Because I've forgotten it again,' was the sullen reply. 'And before you say anything else, be quiet.'

'I'm not laughing yet,' warned the shark. 'As a riddle, yours is beginning to sound lousier and lousier.'

'Please forgive us,' butted in the anxious sardine. 'It seems my partner's mind has become a blank. But if I may be allowed to skim over the rest of the riddle, the punchline is, "That though these twins are like chalk and cheese, still they love each other very much."'

'I know that,' yelled the dolphin. 'Could I help it if that shark made me nervous? My line was on the tip of my tongue. Was it my fault that my heart was also in my mouth? Never skim over my line again. Just say your own and be quiet, be quiet, be quiet.'

'And you be quiet,' said the sardine, just as rudely angry.

Completely ignoring the watching and listening mission members, the Mirth Twins began to argue. It was a loud and moving, bitter war of words. It raged under Toby's wrinkled nose. It stormed in and out the serpent's coloured coils. It even thrashed within centimetres of the shark's sharp, gap-toothed grin. Each twin accused the other of ruining their seventh Farewell Comeback Performance.

'Excuse me,' said Toby, hating to see close

twins fail out. 'If you would stop scrapping for a moment. We don't mind about the ruined riddle, really we don't. What we're concerned about is the love you are wasting in hate. For, win or lose, you will both feel the sadder when you've cooled down, I betcha.'

'I betcha he'll be sadder than I am,' said the breathless sardine, glowering at his large twin.

'Oh, please be quiet, junior twin,' replied the dolphin, nastily. 'Milking sadness is your stock in trade.'

'I can't understand how you can be so close when you fight all the time,' said Toby, shaking his blunt head in wonder. 'How did you ever come together in the first place? You surely didn't meet and shout, "Be quiet," at each other. You must have said hello first.'

'Certainly not goodbye,' agreed the serpent. 'For they wouldn't be together now.'

'Would you like to hear our stories?' said the dolphin, eagerly. He turned to his tiny twin. 'Shall we tell it like it was?'

'You betcha,' came the reply. 'Just make sure you don't forget your lines this time.'

'I won't if you'll please shut up,' the dolphin snapped. Settling comfortably in the green waters he gazed into Toby's wet brown eyes and began. 'Once upon a time a tiny sardine was out swimming with his shoal. Suddenly he turned to speak to his best friend who was swimming just behind. But to his surprise his friend wasn't there. And when the tiny sardine turned back to ask the shoal leader where his best friend had gone, he found that the whole shoal had completely vanished too. He never found out where to. . .'

'You betcha,' grieved the deserted sardine. 'My dad, my mum, my sisters and brothers, my best friend, all were gone leaving me alone in the wide and briny ocean.'

'Did this terrible tragedy happen before tea or after?' questioned the shocked serpent.

'I don't remember,' admitted the sardine, sadly. 'I felt much too lonely to think about grub. But my story is not as sad as my twin's.'

'Oh, please be quiet,' blubbed the dolphin, his blue eyes filling with tears.

But the sardine would not be put off. He immediately launched as sadly into his twin's tale as his twin had launched into his. 'Once upon a time a young dolphin was gambolling happily through the waves with his family when a ship appeared on the horizon and began to steam slowly towards them. . .'

'A whaling ship, I'll bet,' interrupted Toby, angrily. 'My grandad Old Moby Dick still has nightmares about whaling ships. That's why I'm determined to smash up every one I see.'

'Shh,' shushed the raptly listening serpent. 'These life-stories are even sadder than my own. Please continue, you poor little mite.'

'. . .innocently the dolphin family began to

frolic in the bow-wave of the ship,' went on the red-eyed sardine. His voice rose dramatically. 'Then all at once cruel nets were cast overboard, trapping the dolphins in a squirming, silver bundle. Then they were sailed away to be jailed in an artificial sea, doomed to spend the rest of their days performing silly tricks.'

'In return for their tea,' guessed the serpent, his yellow eyes angry. 'Who could even glance at tea while imprisoned?'

'You betcha,' grimaced the sardine. Then he brightened. 'But as you see my twin managed to slip the net and escape. It was then that we met, both alone and in need of cheering up. From that moment we vowed to put our grief behind us and form a comedy act. In that way we could enjoy some happiness by spreading it amongst others.'

'With our jokes and japes and juggling,' nodded the dolphin. Then his comical, bulbous nose drooped miserably. 'But the folk in the Great Wide Bay never took to our act. They greeted us with jeers instead of cheers. That is why we keep retiring from show business then coming back. We hope that one of our farewell comeback performances will click with the public. But alas, still they jeer. I think it's my twin's fault. He just isn't funny enough.'

'Be quiet,' shouted the sardine, furiously. 'At least I always remember my lines. If you aren't

careful I'll forget how much I love you and go solo.'

'You, go solo?' scoffed the dolphin. 'You'd be lost without my really funny backing. I only stick around because I feel sorry for you.'

'Stop torturing each other, Mirth Twins,' cried Toby as the pair began to squabble and brawl again. 'You can't spend your lives shouting, "Be quiet," at each other.'

'You betcha,' agreed the sardine, panting heavily. 'So tell my twin to pack it in. He knows I'm just as anxious as him to perform our act on the Great Wide Bay with everyone clapping instead of sneering.'

'But it's only a dream,' said the dolphin, snuffling through his comical nose. 'Folk will never give us a chance to make them weep with laughter.'

'And to think I felt hard done by having to take tea alone,' said the sorrowful serpent. 'After listening to the sad stories of the Mirth Twins I say we should help them all we can.'

'And to think I've been fretting about a sprained wing,' said the petrel, also deeply moved. 'At least I'll heal, while the hurt of the Mirth Twins never will. I second the serpent's suggestion. We must help them make their act a big success.'

'And to think I threatened to attack their third-rate double-act,' mourned the shark. 'Well, for the first time in my life I've found out something that doesn't have a meal on the bottom line. The Mirth Twins say that this is their seventh Farewell Comeback Performance? Well, according to my sums they are due for a lucky roll of the dice. I'm pleased to announce that the number seven is the luckiest number in the ocean this year.'

'So,' pondered Toby. 'You all think we should help the Mirth Twins in their bid for fame in the Great Wide Bay? Even though my cousins will be gathered there to snigger at our mission when we swim in without an iceberg for them to lick on?'

'I think we should,' said the serpent, stubbornly. 'Even if your cousins refuse to give us tea.'

'Too right,' said the stormy petrel, stoutly. 'I'm prepared to brave any insults in support of these poor comics.'

'Count me in, too,' said the shark, smoothly. 'So long as the lucky numbers are running our way, I'm glad to tag along. Of course, if the unlucky ones begin to stack up against us, I must be allowed to count myself out again.'

'We'd be so grateful for your help,' said the dolphin, his blue eyes gazing pleadingly into Toby's wet brown ones.

'You betcha,' cried the sardine, his tiny red ones glowing hopefully.

'Which leaves me sticking out alone,' remarked Toby, grave-faced. But then his blubbery nose creased into a huge grin. 'Which is a lie, of course. I know what my beloved grandad would do in this situation. He would help others, even though his own dream had melted away like mine. So, Mr Pilot, cling tight to the end of my nose and set a course for the Great Wide Bay.'

'I'm afraid we have a problem there, young Captain,' interrupted the bird, his worried black eyes staring in that direction. 'If we forge ahead we are bound to run into the ship that is forging right at us.'

Everyone looked, their hearts sinking. The bird wasn't lying. A fast-moving smudge was definitely bearing down on the mission.

'It's not a little black cloud this time, that's for sure,' yelled the serpent, his long spiky tail quaking with fear. 'Quick, Shark, you are the speediest. Dart forward and investigate the danger.'

The shark's film-star face turned suddenly shifty. 'Sorry,' he murmured. 'I'm afraid I must play the numbers game and slip away for forty-five minutes and twenty-six seconds, which is precisely how long it takes a whaling ship to make mincemeat of most missions. But I promise to search the sea for bits of you all when I return.' And he knifed away like the coward he was.

Frozen with fear, the serpent and the Mirth Twins, plus Toby with the bird clinging to the end of his nose, waited for their fate to be decided.

'Why,' said the serpent, pointing out something very strange. 'The whaling ship is wearing my colours. See its rainbow coat?'

'It's certainly not ugly black like your usual whaling ship,' agreed the petrel. 'In fact it looks quite a friendly ship. Perhaps we are getting all in a lather about nothing, young Captain?'

But the young captain wasn't listening. 'No whaling ships in this ocean,' he bellowed, finding his courage. 'Attack my mission at your peril. . .' Then, shutting tight his wet brown eyes, he revved up his tail and fins to full throttle. Crashing forward at full speed ahead, he determined to do or die in battle; the petrel, also fired up, shouted closing directions from his perch on Toby's hooter, his beak pointing like a spear at the enemy head.

With a loud and crunching thud Toby's blunt nose struck the ship in the bow, creating a large dent in its brightly painted hull. At once the vessel began to ring bells and toot whistles in alarm. Quickly the young white whale backed off and charged again, this time causing the ship to keel over and rock dangerously. By this time the serpent had also joined the battle.

'No ships,' he cried. 'Leave my friend alone. . .prepare to be stung to death. . .' and he hurled his writhing coils about the ship, his

stinged tail lashing and striking wildly.

Strangely, the battle was very one-sided. The battered ship made no move to fire a lethal harpoon. In fact, it kindly turned in the sea each time Toby charged as if trying to protect his nose from injury on its sharp bits. But in the white heat of battle Toby and the serpent couldn't have realised that the ship was absolutely on their side. Even in calm mood they wouldn't have known that the rainbow-painted vessel was a Greenpeace ship completely in love with whales, and serpents, and stormy petrels, and comical Mirth Twins... even cunning sharks too. Dented and listing from Toby's blows, it turned around in the water and limped off at full speed, its hooters and bells sounding out a joyful chorus as if congratulating the hard-breathing friends on their triumph. With a final warm blast from its hooter, it wobbled over the horizon.

'And don't come back,' yelled Toby, flushed with victory.

'It will be your last goodbye if you do,' bawled the hot and spent serpent.

'We certainly did for that whaler, young Captain,' said the gleeful petrel. 'As a team, we could take on a fleet of whaling ships. How I love a good scrap...'

The Mirth Twins weren't looking at all amused when the fighters returned. But then, having suffered so much in their young lives, they hated violence. Also they were anxious to know whether Toby would still keep his word about boosting their sagging careers in the Great Wide Bay.

'Forty-five minutes and twenty-six seconds precisely,' said the shark who had returned back on time. 'Except, of course, I backed the wrong horse. May I offer my total admiration. . . ?'

'You may,' said a voice quite close at hand. 'But there are horses for courses, and this one is on Great Wide Bay business. And if any one of you dares to call me dinkily pretty I'll scream.'

'But you are dinkily beautiful,' gasped Toby, the battle behind him, his interest now focused on the owner of the voice. 'So tell us, what Great Wide Bay business are you on, for we are bound there.'

'To lay our cards on the table,' grinned the shark. 'So, tell me, pretty sea-horse, are there any more at home like you?'

'Mind your own business,' snapped the blushing she-sea-horse. 'I have been sent from the whales of the Great Wide Bay to enquire why you lot are cluttering up the entrance to their harbour. Are you coming in, or not? If you are coming in, why? If you aren't coming in, also why? The great whales want an answer. . .and please. . .no cracks about my breathtaking beauty. And if you're bursting to know how I manage to move through the ocean in this up-tight manner, mind your own business again.'

'I say we tell this dinky stranger to come back after tea,' said the serpent, indignantly.

'Me and my twin aren't impressed in the least,' said the dolphin, jealously. 'That she-sea-horse uses clever magic to move through the ocean. It's all an illusion. Me and my twin have tricks in our bag just as ocean-shattering. I don't know why she doesn't storm to the very top of show business and be done with it.'

'You betcha,' said the sardine, moodily.

'The little bobbing envoy is certainly better-looking than the shark,' said the serpent, happily. 'Probably because it's still got all its own front teeth.'

'"Her" front teeth,' corrected the prim sea-horse. She looked at Toby. 'So, what message do I take to the whales in the Great Wide Bay? Are you coming in, or not? And why, for I can't see a present or anything? And the whales in our bay always expect presents from strangers who come bobbing in.'

'Well, pretty little bobber,' said the petrel, annoyed. 'You can bob back and tell your whales that this mission will come in when we're good and ready. And if we sail in with nothing then that's their bad luck.'

'We will be coming in with good wishes, though,' said Toby, trying to repair the damage. 'From my beloved grandad Moby Dick who is famous everywhere. We hope the whales in your bay will settle for that?'

'We'll see,' replied the pretty she-sea-horse, bobbing back to the Great Wide Bay on the tip of her tail. 'And don't dare any of you shout, "Goodbye beautiful," after me. I am a very serious envoy, after all.'

'And we are a very serious mission,' shouted Toby, after her. 'We might have failed a bit, but we've still got our pride.'

At his firm words the happiest bunch of failures in the seven seas burst into wild cheers and much clapping of fins. How proud old Moby Dick would have been of his grandson at that moment. What with Toby's acceptance of the loss of his iceberg, the battle with the ship, and the loyalty to his new friends, the young whale was becoming a worthy chip off the old block, having tasted a bit of responsibility.

'Hurrah for sending off the gorgeous envoy with a flea in her ear,' cried the serpent, tangling himself up in his coils in his excitement. 'So let's get cracking on the singing lessons. If the Mirth Twins are quick learners we'll arrive in the Great Wide Bay in time to watch her take her haughty tea, with nobody invited.'

'That's another decision I've made,' said Toby, resolved. 'From this time on everyone will be allowed to sing their own songs. The Mirth Twins, who will be leading our failed but still proud mission into the Great Wide Bay can sing their personal song as we sail in. You do have a personal song, Mirth Twins?'

'You betcha,' shouted the chuffed sardine, his red eyes sparkling. 'It's a belter of a song. Just wait until you hear the cracking way I sing it.'

'Cracked more like,' snapped the dolphin. 'You could never carry a tune or a beat. Just hum, and let me deal with the melody. For I've rehearsed our song down to the last tiny quaver.'

'Shut up,' glowered the sardine.

'Then prepare to sing it with feeling, Dolphin,' cried Toby. 'And you, Sardine, prepare to hum it as if it were the greatest sea-symphony. The rest of us will learn it as we go along, and join in at the top of our voices. Are you ready, Mr Pilot, have you got a fix on the lie of the land?'

'My sensitive beak is quivering like a compass-needle. It's pointed directly along the prim track left by the delightful she-sea-horse-envoy, young Captain,' shrilled the bird from the tip of Toby's nose. 'It's itching to steer this mission into the Great Wide Bay where the jeers and sneers await us. But are we down-hearted. . . ?'

'Never,' yelled Toby. 'Okay, Mirth Twins, full speed ahead to where the bird said, and let me hear the full blast of that song of yours.'

93

Excitedly gambolling ahead, the Mirth Twins sped off in the direction indicated by the petrel's quivering beak, Toby and the serpent and the grinning shark in convoy behind. Never had the stormy petrel felt so proud as he steered Toby and his friends into the Great Bay, his feathers fluttering in the wind. How cocksure he felt, a little lame bird coming home a hero, and bang on course. But it was the personal song of the Mirth Twins that surprised everyone, especially Toby.

As the party approached the great sweep of land with its dense fringe of coconut palms and banana trees, as it turned to enter the Great Wide Bay where the southern whales sported and spouted, so the twins burst into their joyous, personal song. It was a simple song. Some would say it was a silly song. But it was a happy song, and easy to learn as all the best songs are. Toby and his mission had no trouble learning the words and the tune, for they were as familiar as could be. So familiar that Toby, pausing for breath after the third rendering of it, felt forced to speak his puzzled mind.

'But of course it's your song, young whale,' answered the happy dolphin. 'But it's also everybody's song. When folk want to express joy at being alive, they sing the song that comes naturally to them. But just listen to the waiting residents of the Great Wide Bay. They have opened their hearts and are singing our song too. Praise be that they've finally found their voices and senses of humour. But pardon me, for I expect that my fan club is dying to see my thrilling over-the-shoulder-backward-leap. I only hope that my ears can stand the deafening roars of "more" when I've completed it.' And he bored beneath the sea to get a good run-up for his death-defying leap from the waves, the sardine shouting "you betcha" as he also dived down in preparation for leaping even higher than his twin.

As he sailed through the Great Wide Bay, Toby enjoyed to the full the first mass welcome he'd ever received in his life. He didn't care a jot that others had taken over his favourite song as if it were theirs. It sounded wonderful whoever sang it. As he and his mission cruised through the narrow straights they were almost blasted out of the water by the full-throated roar of:

> 'We all live in a lovely wavy sea,
> A lovely wavy sea,
> A lovely wavy sea,
> We all live in a lovely wavy sea. . .'

'. . .Wide enough for you and me. . .but not ships. . .' bawled Toby, blissfully happy as the host of Great Wide Bay singers paused in mid-note to allow him to sing the last line on his own. And, blessedly, in that crowded and sparkling bay there was not even the suggestion of a little black cloud to marr the blue horizon, to spoil the occasion, to blight the sea.

7
BEHOLD, THE JOYFUL SEA

Without the merest sliver of an iceberg to his name, Toby proudly coasted in to face what he believed would be the wrath and scorn of his southern cousins. With the joking and japing and juggling Mirth Twins stealing all the thunder he led his mission through the emerald waters of a bay chock-a-block full of residents doing what they liked doing best...being happy.

Schools of flying-fish arced like a firework display over Toby's blunt, grinning nose. Fat seals, forming a guard of honour on either side of him, honked and clapped their flippers in appreciation. Along the palm-fringed sandy shore, cliques of pink crabs clacked their claws to the beat of 'everybody's song', while around the bay wobbled a glob of loudly singing jellyfish, their painful stings packed away for the day. And above all wheeled the sea-birds, shrieking in astonishment as they spotted the long-lost stormy petrel posing proudly on his young captain's nose. Then suddenly the Mirth Twins ceased their joking and japing and juggling. Confident that they had won every happy heart in the bay with their comedy routine, they leapt high into the air in a triumphant victory V before swimming aside to catch their breath, but also to allow Toby to swim into the limelight.

With the petrel murmuring encouragement, Toby flippered the last few metres to come face to face with an old whale who looked uncannily like his grandad back home. Clustered about by his adoring family, the old one spoke in a slow and gentle voice.

'Welcome, young Toby, from the tip of Iceland,' he said. 'My little she-sea-horse messenger warned us of your coming. I'm sorry she isn't here to announce your arrival herself, but she's bobbed off in a huff. She is still angry that your mission called her merely beautiful when she felt her clever mind should have been praised. But never mind, we are very pleased to see the grandson of my cousin the famous Moby Dick in our waters.'

'But does he deserve our welcome?' shouted a small whale with slate-blue eyes. 'When folk visit other folk, they usually bring a gift as a present. So where's this Toby's present for us? He could at least have brought us a cold iceberg from his cold home for us to play with.'

'Be quiet,' butted in the dolphin, cruising close to deal the cheeky youngster a sharp blow on his blunt nose.

'You betcha,' cried the sardine, his little red eyes glaring as he also butted the forward youngster. 'What do you know about going without presents? I could tell you a sad story about a dolphin who hasn't even the presence of his family.'

'And I could tell you the lonely tale of a sardine who lost the gift of love when his shoal deserted him,' cried the hot-tempered dolphin.

'But you both won't. . .I hope. . . ?' interrupted the gentle old whale. 'For I'm still waiting for my small relative to say how pleased he is to see us.'

'And I am. . .I am,' blurted Toby, humbly. 'I have long yearned for this moment, Southern Grandad.'

'Then where are your gifts as presents for us?' shouted the rude young whale, again. 'You'd soon complain if you left without one.'

'My friend can explain if you'll let him,' shouted the angry serpent. 'Do you think he'd visit his southern grandad without carefully choosing a present to bring?'

'In other words, be quiet,' cried the Mirth Twins. 'At the risk of you all sneering at our next performance, we won't tell you again.'

All this valiant defence of him caused Toby to dissolve into tears. His wet brown eyes became all puffy as his misery spilled over.

'Dry your eyes and tell how it was, young Captain,' cried the bird. 'Tell these fat layabouts what our mission went through to arrive here with nothing.'

'I truly did have a gift when I set out to see you, Southern Grandad,' blurted Toby, raising his saggy blunt head. 'It was the tallest, bluest, brightest iceberg in the whole of the northern seas. But, alas, the hot sun and the many delays we suffered on our journey reduced it to nothing. Now I am racked with guilt. If you and your angry family die from thirst it will be all my fault. So, Southern Grandad, if you wish to punish me before you die from thirst, I won't blame you at all.'

'There, there, lad,' murmured the kindly old whale with a twinkle. 'Things aren't so bad as they seem. We hot, southern whales usually get over our water problems.'

'Then why are the tongues of us young ones lolling out?' shouted the young whale, pursuing his jokey torment of Toby, much to the amusement of his fellows. He rolled dramatically on to his back, gasping, 'I'm going. . .I'm going. . .for pity's sake. . .give me an iceberg to lick on. . .'

The old whale was just about to chide him for his silliness when he was interrupted again.

'I refuse to let my friend Toby take the blame,' cried the loyal serpent, his yellow eyes flashing. 'If I hadn't kept suggesting stops for tea, our mission would have arrived here with the iceberg in mint condition. No, Southern Grandad, the blame for your family's raging thirst is mostly mine.'

'If I could say a few words. . .' said the gentle old whale. But he wasn't allowed to.

'Hang on,' butted in the indignant petrel. 'I won't have my captain and that silly serpent hogging all the blame. I insist that my third-rate steering is scoffed at. Because of my love for all points of the compass our mission went round in more than one aimless circle. So, Southern Grandad, punish me for the loss of Toby's iceberg. Here is my breast. Tear out my feathers one by one and still I'll cry that I'm mostly to blame.'

'If a southern grandad could say a few words. . .' the weary old whale tried again. But once more he was interrupted. This time by the cunning shark.

'I figure a fraction of the blame is mine, Southern Grandad,' he said, grudgingly. 'While the young whale and that vicious serpent were straining to push the iceberg south, I was only pretending to. But a point in my favour, it was I who cleared a gap in the salmon ranks for our mission to sail through, squeamish though it made me feel. But the largest sum of guilt must be totted up in other columns. Was it my fault that our leader kept dashing off to bash little black clouds? Was it my fault that the serpent was always whining about stopping for tea, and bashing the front teeth out of honest sharks? Was it my fault that our pilot happened to be a stupid bird who wouldn't know a straight line if he tripped over one? So, Southern Grandad, when you come to dish out blame I hope you'll appreciate my small percentage of it. . . OWCH. . . OWCH. . . why am I always attacked when I'm trying to be sincere. . . ?'

'You cunning, lying scoundrel,' cried a usually quiet young whale who had been listening carefully to every word. Breathing and spouting heavily, he justified his impulsive act of violence. 'I struck the rest of your teeth from your smile because I hate your film-star smarm. You are nothing but an extremely handsome liar and cheat, and killer to boot. So, never again try to throw most of the blame for anything on to our lovely cousin from the north, and his friends the loyal serpent and the dizzy-headed bird. We southern whales are completely in their corner, aren't we, Southern Grandad?'

'So was I...sometimes...' lisped the shocked shark, spitting out yet more teeth. 'I shall be very glad when "Be Kind To Sharks" week comes around again. It's the only time I'm certain of not being smashed in the gob.'

'Good or wicked, we all have our good days,' smiled wise old Southern Grandad, allowed to speak at last. His kind grey eyes focused on the nervous Toby. 'To fail in a mission is not the end of the world, small relative, it's the trying that's important. And you,' he soothed, 'you tried to carry it through, that's the main thing. And you were bound to fail anyway, for icebergs never did travel well. Sly Old Moby must have known that. But take heart, young Toby, for the old rascal was testing you for your own good. And you've certainly passed the courage and endurance test with flying colours. For you didn't slink back home when your gift for us melted into the sea. As for us being angry, don't worry. We southern whales always manage to get by on the few drops of water we glean from our huge ocean. So, now that the serious business is over, I suggest we indulge in a bit of light-heartedness. I think a celebration for you and your friends is in order here.'

'If you'll permit me, Southern Grandad,' snapped a honey-toned voice. It was her, the little she-sea-horse-cum-secretary, trying to sound brisk and efficient. She bobbed primly from behind a dozy turtle where she'd been hiding and listening. Primly, she said, 'I agree. . .a light-hearted celebration is just the thing for these weary travellers from the north. I suggest a large tea-party. If I may be permitted to organize it in my usual business-like fashion, Southern Grandad. . . ?'

'I certainly won't allow it,' shouted the happy serpent. 'You are much too delicate and gorgeous to rustle up a huge tea on your own. I insist on doing the hard fetching and carrying of the various ingredients. Don't protest, for I've always wanted to do something gallant. I'm sure you'd be better employed bobbing prettily on the sidelines.'

At his chauvinistic words the ravishing she-sea-horse scuttled back behind the snoring turtle to have another temper tantrum.

'A spot of tea it shall be then,' said Southern Grandad. 'For our visitors must be ravenous after their long journey.'

'Thank you very much, sir, Southern Grandad,' said Toby, vastly relieved. 'We could do with something nourishing before we begin the long northwards journey home. We are all anxious to get back to our own dear seas again, you'll understand.'

'Please, not all of us,' begged the serpent who had just returned from the depths with his claws full of delicious kelp-weed for a starter. 'If it won't break your heart, Toby my friend, may I stay here in the south? What with all the lovely sunshine and kind new friends to invite for tea, I'll never need to ever shout goodbye again. Please wish me well and let me stay here where my life will be one long tea-time. Don't condemn me to return to my lonely patch of foam where the only "hello" is my own, thrown back on the biting cold winds.'

'Of course you should stay where your heart is, Serpent,' said Toby, hiding his sadness at losing his first best friend. 'You deserve to spend the rest of your life sunning yourself and shouting hello when folk drop in for tea. But me and the stormy petrel will never forget you as we travel north towards the cold seas of my home.'

'Oh, dear,' murmured the petrel, awkwardly. 'I'm afraid I must beg out too, young Captain. You see, I was born and raised in these warm seas. Here is home for me. I only fly north for kicks. . .say once a year. But as you paddle northwards without me I'll often think warmly of the firm nose you offered as a perch when I was in peril on the sea.' Toby nodded in tearful understanding, his wet brown eyes finally turning to gaze in hope at the remaining member of his ill-fated mission.

'I don't know why you're looking at me,' remarked the shark, alarmed. 'My excuse for staying here is as good as anybody's. In fact I've decided to settle here and teach mathematics. I plan to open a Master Class for flying-fish who want to learn why their numbers are getting fewer and fewer each year. I reckon those flashing little beggars are in need of a few sharp lessons in subtraction.'

Toby made no comment, for he was becoming used to being turned down. His wrinkled nose barely snuffled as yet another deserter spoke.

'And we Mirth Twins would be fools to risk taking our comedy act on tour in the north,' shouted the now-famous dolphin. 'You saw how warmly these southern folk took to my new comedy routines.'

'*My* new comedy routines,' corrected the red-eyed sardine, his short temper flaring. 'My southern fans only applauded your up-and-under leaps out of sympathy.'

'Oh, *please* be quiet,' yelled his partner, charging forward to chase his twin in and out of the school of astonished whales. They were still hurling threats at each other while everyone else was enjoying a really slap-up tea. They didn't care that the sun was supper-time setting over the Great Wide Bay. For being very sensible they all knew that anytime was the proper time for tea. And what a tea it was. Even the angry she-sea-horse, who had come out of hiding from behind the snoozing turtle, agreed that it was a pity such a meal had to end. But it did. . .just after midnight. Then suddenly,

Toby felt the urge to go. For not only was the cold north calling him, but he was missing his beloved grandad more than words could say.

'Thank you for your hospitality, and for being so understanding, Southern Grandad,' he said, his wet brown eyes suddenly misting over with homesickness. 'But now I'm very anxious to start for home. Is there a message you'd like me to deliver to my own northern grandad?'

'I'd like to send him a gift in return for the one we didn't receive,' replied the old whale, his grey eyes sparkling with mischief. 'Not an iceberg of course, for those are in short supply down here. But tell me, how are my old sparring partner's eyes these days?'

'Well, Grandad Moby does squint and peer a bit,' admitted Toby. 'And he does bellow, "Great thundering icebergs," when he bumps into rocks off the tip of Iceland that he didn't see were there.'

'In that case, I have just the gift as a present for him,' said the other, smiling. 'I just happen to have four spare pilot-fish who are unemployed at the moment. I'm sure my old cousin will find them useful to guide him around dangerous objects on dark nights. Would he like them, do you think?'

'I'll bet he'll love 'em, Southern Grandad,' answered an eager Toby. 'And I promise to deliver your kind gift safely home. It will be like another mission for me. Thank you so much for entrusting the pilot-fish to my care, especially when my first mission melted away to nothing. I am ready to take charge of Grandad's new seeing-aids whenever they are ready to travel.'

There was a loud commotion and much splashing from behind the old whale's huge bulk. Presently the she-sea-horse appeared shepherding four very slim and extremely boisterous small fish. Toby gazed worriedly at them. Judging by all the fuss they were making, they didn't seem cut out for guiding at all. From what he could see their main aim seemed to be trying to swim in different directions from each other. But he stifled his doubts as the old whale spoke again.

'Now, young Toby,' he smiled. 'Do you still think you can deliver my gift? But whether you do or whether you don't, you can tell Old Moby Dick that he's raised a grandson to be proud of. In fact, such a grand little chap that I'm tempted to pinch you for my own, and keep you here.'

'I couldn't possibly stay, Southern Grandad,' said Toby, horrified. 'Would you mind being my second favourite grandad, and let me go. Only I'm anxious to carry out your orders and get back home where my first grandad is bound to be pining away for me.' So saying, he nosed and flippered the squabbling pilot-fish into a line-ahead position. They immediately streaked off in four different directions. But the fishes hadn't reckoned on Toby being made of very determined stuff indeed. They had another thing coming if they thought they could humiliate him in front of his grinning cousins. Cheered to the echo by his many admirers in the Great Wide Bay, Toby badgered and bullied, cajoled and thumped the protesting foursome towards the open sea.

'Good luck, Toby my friend,' shouted the serpent, his yellow eyes streaming tears. 'May you enjoy many tea-times as you battle northwards. Forgive me when I don't cry goodbye, for only "hello" can express my love for you. So hello, dear companion, until we surely meet again.'

'Smooth sailing, and watch your barnacles and your binnacles, young Captain,' yelled the stormy petrel. In his excitement he dug his sharp claws into Southern Grandad's blubbery nose, his new, safe berth. He screamed on, 'Remember, always make sure that the sun rises over your right flipper. Then you'll know you are bang on course for home, or do I mean the left flipper. . . ?'

'And if you meet up with the Silver Streak again, give 'em a taste of guts and gore,' roared the bloodthirsty shark. At least he tried to roar. But in fact his voice was now a very attractive lisp as he gave out terrible advice through the double-gap in his once-handsome smile.

'And may the funny jokes of the Mirth Twins crowd your mind,' cried the dolphin and the sardine. 'And may you have fun every splash of the way home, for splashing alone through a lonely sea can be very sad if you're miserable.'

Their encouraging shouts died away as Toby urged his quarrelling charges through the night, bound for home and desperate to see his beloved grandad once more.

8
SINGING, SAILING HOME

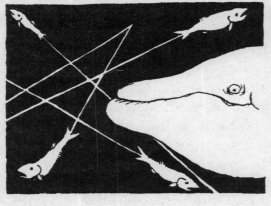

The sea was kind to a young white whale as he wallowed home. The waves were gentle roller-coasters that felt delightful to slide up and down on. The weather loved Toby too. The nights were moonlit with plenty of stars, and the dawns were blue with the promise of sun and fair sailing. Even the horizons Toby fearfully scanned remained blessedly empty. Not one ugly whaling ship appeared to blight the serene beauty of the sea. Though grateful for these kindnesses, Toby more and more yearned to feel the sharp northern winds buffeting his nose, the cold sleeting rain hammering shut his squinting eyes. For only then would he feel that his long journey was almost over, the tip of Iceland merely over the last horizon.

He wasn't alone in wishing that he was somewhere else. Weeks of being pushed north in a perfect straight line had made the pilot-fish mutinous. They hated being treated as a gift for a grandad not even their own. But Toby didn't seem to understand that pilot-fish had hopes and dreams and feelings too. He didn't even invite them to share tea with the new friends he met on the way. Shooed aside, the four fuming fishes had to endure the lip-smacking of a pompous sea-lion who between gulps, boasted about his royal relatives in Africa. They seethed as Toby listened sympathetically to a titchy, but ferocious crab who declared with relish that his hobby was hunting down and devouring peace-loving sharks, the liar. But their fury spilled over into revolt when Toby entertained a slob of a giant octopus. For after slobbering down three helpings of sea-porcupine he had the nerve to slide his shifty black eyes in their direction, and say:

'They look tasty, I must say. I'm very partial to pilot-fish. So shall we tuck in. . . ?'

After Toby had hastily explained that the shivering fishes were a gift for his grandad and wished his slimy guest goodbye, the irate pilot-fish let him have it with all their stored-up grievances.

113

'Why do you treat us in this shoddy way?' cried their spokesman. 'Don't we count as lawful residents of the sea? You do a lot of singing about "all living in a lovely wavy sea", so why do you treat us as though we have no rights to also enjoy our lives? Why should we pilot-fish be parcelled out as presents? I'll have you know we four also have a song that we composed from our hearts.'

His fellow prisoners chorused their angry agreement.

'I beg your pardon, pilot-fish,' said Toby, quite astonished. 'I didn't realise that you felt so strongly, and were also musical. So could I hear your song, the better to understand your point of view?'

'Just so long as you don't suffer from dizzy spells,' he was warned. 'Because some folk keel upside-down with their heads in a spin during our "Everywhichway" song. But if you insist, I'll sing it. While I'm doing so my friends will be performing the exciting "Everywhichway" dance. But be warned, take a tight grip on your nerves in case their wild dancing should drive you into a boogieing frenzy. So are you prepared?'

Toby nodded nervously as he prepared to fight off a dizzy, boogieing spell, his flippers tucked tightly into his tubby body.

'Let it rip then,' cried the singer, already beginning to boogie in the water. At the same

114

time his three friends began to zip around in circles and squares and triangles as he broke into song:

'As presents we don't please,
As gifts we are a bore,
So if we swim off different ways
We hope you won't be sore.
If He swims to the sun,
And Him swims to the moon,
If She swims home to the Great Wide Bay,
While I swim everywhichway.'

It was a dizzying song and dance indeed. At the end of it Toby found himself charging about the sea as frenziedly as the pilot-fish. Frankly, he blamed it on the boogie. As he recovered his senses he began to feel a deep shame. What right had he to treat the four freedom-loving fishes as a package of goods to be delivered to his grandad? It just wasn't right. Having made their point the pilot-fish waited for Toby's reaction, their eyes gleaming with the hint of more rebellion if his heart didn't soften towards their cause.

'I apologise, Pilot-fish,' he said, humbly. 'I should have realised that your freedom is just as important as anybody's. And to think that I've forced you all this way against your will.'

'It was only because we liked you that we didn't vanish like quicksilver ages ago,' said the spokesman, angrily. 'Didn't you ever realise that you were shoving along with the end of your nose a ticking bomb that could have exploded in your face?'

'I didn't,' answered Toby, horrified.

'If you had only tried the kind approach from the start,' bristled He who fancied the sun.

'If you had only begged us to come north with you,' agreed Him who favoured the moon, his expression radiant with hurt.

'If you had only said that your grandad was a gift for us, instead of us being a gift for him,' pouted She, still toying with the idea of swimming straight home to the Great Wide Bay.

'In plain words, if only you had asked us to volunteer our services,' said the singer, plaintively. 'If you had we might have quite liked the idea of being the guiding companions for your doddery old grandad. So how do you answer our demand for freedom? And be warned, answer wrongly and you won't see our fins for bubbles.'

Toby's wet brown eyes suddenly filled with sincere tears. 'Pilot-fish, from the bottom of my heart I beg you to volunteer to become the eyes and ears of my famous old grandad who is no longer the young blade he was.'

'And we immediately volunteer for the post,' chorused the pilot-fish. 'For Old Moby has always been a hero to freedom-lovers like us.'

116

'Thank you,' replied Toby, deeply moved. 'And could you volunteer just one more little thing for me? Because I want Grandad to be proud of me, would you volunteer to sing my song instead of yours, as we cruise into home waters? After all, as I learned in the south, my song is really everybody's song.'

'Are you seriously asking us to volunteer twice?' gasped the singer pilot-fish. He frowned. 'This is quite unheard of. I'm afraid we'll have to negotiate again. Will you excuse us while we withdraw and consider?'

'Withdraw and consider as long as you want,' said Toby. Then anxiously, 'But not for too long, I hope, for I'm desperate to get home.'

The pilot-fish swam aside and went into a huddle. In the meantime night fell. Cold and frosty, the hours passed slowly. Toby could only wait patiently as the pilot-fish deliberated their decision, his wet brown anxious eyes fixed intently on the Northern Lights that flashed and danced over the last horizon where lay his Icelandic home. Wallowing and wishing, he hoped and hoped that everything would come right with every beat of his huge heart.

Only the occasional spouting of a whale disturbed the peace just off the tip of Iceland. But for one, the abundance of peace and quiet was wearing a bit thin.

'My, but I do feel lonely,' sighed Old Moby Dick to the surging sea and the sky. To relieve his boredom he slapped the still waters with his mighty tail, then cocked a gloomy eye over his massive shoulder to view the reaction. But the roosting sea-birds were used to his sighing and tail-slapping. They merely adjusted their webbed feet on his back, and closed their eyes more tightly shut.

'Lonely and bored, that's me,' the old whale sighed again. He voiced his grumbles to a herd of basking seals who were sleepily lolling in the shade of his flipper. 'I mean, can you imagine not playing a lively game in ages, nor singing a silly song? Shall I tell you how long it's been since I played a game or sang a song. . . ?'

Yawning rudely, the irritated seals slid rapidly away to find a more peaceful basking spot. In their opinions there was nothing more boring than a bored old whale, famous or not. Old Moby was just about to sigh and slap his tail again, to annoy the sea-birds, when his ears pricked to a familiar sound. Faintly he could hear the strains of his grandson's 'wavy sea' song, and sounding like it was being sung by a full choir. He was just about to roll over in the sea with joy when there was a rapid swirling in the sea nearby. Too late Old Moby Dick tried to take avoiding action. In that instant he suddenly received a rib-buckling thump in his side.

'Great thundering icebergs, I've been scuttled again,' he bellowed, wincing with pain, but delighted just the same.

'And it serves you right, Grandad,' cried Toby surfacing, a wide grin on his blunt face. 'How many times have you warned me to always stay alert, yet I've caught you napping again?'

'It's young Toby lad, home from the sea,' shouted the happiest old whale in any of the seven seas. 'I knew he wouldn't forget his grandad. I knew he wouldn't desert him. I knew he would come back home one day.'

'Of course, Grandad,' whooped a joyous Toby. 'Didn't you often tell me that the best thing about sailing is the coming home? But listen, Grandad, I'm worried about your eyes and your ears. I'm worried that I caught you napping too easily. Now, I have the perfect solution to your problem. If you will glance in the water near your nose you will see four little. . .'

'So, how did your mission go down in the south?' interrupted Grandad, his tone filled with equal mixtures of happiness and curiosity. 'Don't tell me your mission succeeded. It was only a mischievous test, after all.'

'The iceberg went down very well, Grandad,' replied a sad Toby. 'Just over the equator, actually. It melted away without trace before I could deliver it to our southern cousins. But not to worry, for Southern Grandad congratulated me very warmly for trying my best. And, Grandad, he sent you a gift in return. He said it would help your failing sight and hearing. So, Grandad, may I introduce my four little friends who are not only fans of your famous exploits, but also anxious to volunteer to stop you bumping into sharp bits of ice when you go for your brisk morning swims. Firstly let me present the one who would some day like to swim to the sun.'

'Hang on,' interrupted Old Moby, his eyes peering at the four small splashes, cavorting before his nose. 'Who are these pesky little critters, and what are they doing here, and why are they nudging my nose as if trying to dash me off somewhere. . . ?'

'Pesky?' shouted the spokesman pilot-fish, indignantly. 'Why does our future charge call us "pesky"? Why does our hero peer at us as if we were worthless things without dignity and rights? I. . .we thought we had been "volunteered" here to help an old whale in his dotage. So why does he call us "pesky"?'

'The word "pesky" is an old whale term,' said Toby, hastily. 'It means "very nice". It means that you four and he are going to get on very well.'

'In that case we think he's pesky too,' said the She who sometime back had wanted to swim home to the Great Wide Bay.

'He is a smashing pesky hero, and we are pleased to serve him for ever,' agreed He who could easily have swum off to the sun but for Toby's plea.

'As a grandad worthy of piloting about, he'll do,' announced Him who loved the moon. 'So where does he want to go?'

'Everywhichway, I hope,' said the singer-spokesman pilot-fish. 'So are you ready, Grandad? Just follow us wherever you want to go, for from now on we are your devoted eyes and ears.'

'Pilot-fish? Since when did I need pilot-fish to guide me about?' exploded Old Moby. 'Whose idea of a joke is this?'

'It's no joke, Grandad,' said Toby, shocked and taken aback. 'In fact the pilot-fish are a return gift from Southern Grandad who worries about you very much. A tit-for-tat gift, he called them.'

'If you don't need us, we'll go,' said the angry spokesman pilot-fish, readying himself to swim off everywhichway.

Suddenly Old Moby threw back his enormous head and began to chuckle as he realised that his flipper had been well and truly pulled by his cunning old cousin in the south. Toby and the pilot-fish looked on in puzzlement. They could see nothing funny at all. What could be funny about helping a doddery old whale to swim about the ocean without bumping into ice-floes and things. . . ?

'So where shall we go then?' asked a grinning Old Moby. He glanced mischievously at the now smiling pilot-fish. 'Could you four guide me north towards the Great Ice Pack? Now there's a sight I'd love to see again.'

'We'd only lead you there straight as a die,' chorused his eager helpers. 'And back again, if you want.'

'Singing as we go, of course,' smiled the old whale, glancing at his beloved grandson. 'So what shall we sing, Toby lad?'

'What else but everybody's song?' shouted Toby, happy to be home after his adventures. 'And, Grandad, you can sing the last line of the song on your own, all the way there, and all the way back. How's that then?'

'And afterwards I hope you'll finally swim over here and get a bit of tea down you,' shrilled Toby's mother from the middle of the distant spouting school. 'But I warn you, three seconds late and I'll give it to someone else. To some young whale who appreciates a good filling tea, and arrives in time for it. . .'

But Toby hadn't the time to listen to his mother. He was already ranging alongside his grandad, preparing to try out the old whale's new 'eyes and ears' with a long-distance swim to the Great Ice Pack. With the pilot-fish taking up stations to the fore, and sides, and back of the two whales, the party set off towards another horizon, their song loud on the clear, crisp Arctic air. As their voices joined together in joyous song, so the sea-birds rose shrieking from their perch on a happy old white whale's back. But then, how could they possibly understand that the words of the song were shouted into the air not only as an appeal for whales to be left in peace, but also for the little likes of them who only wished to roost on an old whale's back in peace. But amid the bad-tempered shrieking and fluttering, more than one young bird found himself wheeling and humming as the ponderous party below set out for a distant horizon, singing lustily:

'We all live in a lovely wavy sea,
Wide enough for you and me. . .but not
ships. . .'

The tune and the words died away with distance. But the memory lingered on in the air. . .would one day be whole-heartedly sung in far-flung parts.

Goodday, goodnight, and good luck, Toby and Moby, and everyone in the wavy sea. May you wallow and enjoy tea-time forever.

A Selected List of Fiction from Mammoth

While every effort is made to keep prices low, it is sometimes necessary to increase prices at short notice. Mammoth Books reserves the right to show new retail prices on covers which may differ from those previously advertised in the text or elsewhere.

The prices shown below were correct at the time of going to press.

☐	7497 0366 0	**Dilly the Dinosaur**	Tony Bradman	£1.99
☐	7497 0021 1	**Dilly and the Tiger**	Tony Bradman	£1.99
☐	7497 0137 4	**Flat Stanley**	Jeff Brown	£1.99
☐	7497 0048 3	**Friends and Brothers**	Dick King-Smith	£1.99
☐	7497 0054 8	**My Naughty Little Sister**	Dorothy Edwards	£1.99
☐	416 86550 X	**Cat Who Wanted to go Home**	Jill Tomlinson	£1.99
☐	7497 0166 8	**The Witch's Big Toe**	Ralph Wright	£1.99
☐	7497 0218 4	**Lucy Jane at the Ballet**	Susan Hampshire	£2.25
☐	416 03212 5	**I Don't Want To!**	Bel Mooney	£1.99
☐	7497 0030 0	**I Can't Find It!**	Bel Mooney	£1.99
☐	7497 0032 7	**The Bear Who Stood on His Head**	W. J. Corbett	£1.99
☐	416 10362 6	**Owl and Billy**	Martin Waddell	£1.75
☐	416 13822 5	**It's Abigail Again**	Moira Miller	£1.75
☐	7497 0031 9	**King Tubbitum and the Little Cook**	Margaret Ryan	£1.99
☐	7497 0041 6	**The Quiet Pirate**	Andrew Matthews	£1.99
☐	7497 0064 5	**Grump and the Hairy Mammoth**	Derek Sampson	£1.99

All these books are available at your bookshop or newsagent, or can be ordered direct from the publisher. Just tick the titles you want and fill in the form below.

Mandarin Paperbacks, Cash Sales Department, PO Box 11, Falmouth, Cornwall TR10 9EN.

Please send cheque or postal order, no currency, for purchase price quoted and allow the following for postage and packing:

UK   80p for the first book, 20p for each additional book ordered to a maximum charge of £2.00.

BFPO   80p for the first book, 20p for each additional book.

Overseas   £1.50 for the first book, £1.00 for the second and 30p for each additional book including Eire   thereafter.

NAME (Block letters) ....

ADDRESS ....

....

....